D1526923

THE CLEOPATRA CIPHER

ADRIAN WEST ADVENTURE BOOK 1

L.D. GOFFIGAN

PROLOGUE

Alexandria, Egypt
Royal Palace of the Ptolemies
August 12th, 30 BCE

Cleopatra knew that death was coming for her.

That young Roman upstart, Octavian, was already marching into Alexandria. It was only a matter of time before he would arrive at the palace to seize her and her children.

She had already sent away her eldest, Caesarion, to India with his tutor Rhodon, a man she trusted with her life. Her youngest children, Alexander, Selene, and Ptolemy were here in the palace with her. She had wanted to send them away, but they were still so young, and she had hoped . . .

Despair seized her, but she closed her eyes and willed it away. She was the last ruling Ptolemy, queen of Egypt. She was determined to keep the Ptolemaic legacy alive.

The Ptolemies had ruled over Egypt for centuries, ever since the great Alexander marched his armies into Egypt. She would not be the one to fail them. As long as her children, heirs to the Ptolemaic wealth and legacy, were alive, there was hope of preserving the dynasty.

Now was not the time for despair. Had she not triumphed so many times before? When she was a young woman of twenty-one, her brother-husband had forced her to flee Alexandria. At the advice and counsel of his tutors, he had tried to set her aside and have her killed, to rule Egypt alone. Had she not made Julius Caesar her ally and eventual lover, restoring herself to the throne and holding her position, even as the threat of Rome continued to loom?

She had, and she would triumph again. She had already prepared for this moment, all the while hoping that it would not come to this.

But she still had loyal followers. She still had her beloved children.

Straightening, she moved toward a chest in the corner of her chamber where she kept her most precious jewels. Most had already been spirited away during the war she and Marc Antony had raged against that upstart, but she had kept some pieces with her.

Grief skittered through her at the memory of Antony. What was once an alliance of convenience, as it had been with Caesar, had turned into love. Now he had gone to join the gods, leaving her and their children alone.

She forced away her grief, blinking back tears. She opened the chest, taking in the jewels until her eyes landed on one of the simplest pieces. It was an amethyst ring, passed down to her from the mother she had never known, one that even the most fashion-conscious Roman was likely to overlook. It would fit perfectly on her daughter's finger.

Lifting the ring, she sent a silent prayer to the gods that her plan, long in the making, would work.

Her kingdom, her throne—her family's very survival—depended upon it.

MOMENTS LATER, Cleopatra stood in the center of her chamber, waiting for her children to arrive, after sending her most loyal servant, Charmion, to fetch them.

As they entered, rushing to her, her heart clenched. While her oldest looked like his father Julius Caesar, her youngest three children were the spitting image of her beloved Antony. The twins, her sun and moon, Alexander Helios and Cleopatra Selene, had inherited his dark eyes and curly hair; her baby boy Ptolemy already possessed his beauty that was still so inherently masculine. They would always remind her of him.

She sank down as her children ran into her arms, allowing herself several long moments to rest her cheek against their curls, to stroke their soft skin. Now that all was on the verge of being lost; her children were all she had.

"Mama?" Selene asked, her tear-filled gaze meeting hers. "I overheard the guards. They said the Romans are here, and they're coming to the palace."

Cleopatra met her children's eyes, fighting to keep her own rising panic at bay. Now was not the time to heed her instincts as a mother and soothe them; she had to be honest with them. She did not have much time.

"Yes. The Romans have entered the city; they will be here soon. And that is why I want you to listen carefully to what I am going to tell you."

While her youngest, Ptolemy, was too young to understand, Selene and Alexander listened intently to her words, their eyes wide as they grasped the enormity of what she told them.

When she finished speaking, one of her trusted guards appeared at the door to her chamber.

"My queen," he said, bowing his head respect-fully. "Octavian and his army have arrived at the palace gates. They have sent a messenger ahead. He wishes to meet with you."

Cleopatra gave him a nod, turning back to her children.

"Remember what I have told you, my loves," she said.

"We will," Alexander promised, though his lips trembled. He was trying so hard to appear as strong and brave as a man, but he was still a boy. She reached out to touch his face.

"Give your mother a kiss," she said, trying not to let her voice waver. "I will send for you when I can."

They dutifully kissed her, and she again allowed herself several moments to just breathe them in. Her instincts as a mother and a ruler battled for dominance; the mother in her wanted to hold them and never let them go, the ruler in her knew that they must. She had to force herself to stand, watching as Charmion led them out of her chamber. A sudden unfathomable grief seized her at the thought of never seeing them again.

I will, she thought with determination. *Gods willing, I will.*

She prayed they had heeded what she had told them, and that they would succeed. *They will,* she told herself firmly. *They must.*

Cleopatra turned to the guard, who still hovered in the doorway. She was glad she had taken the time to dress in her finest. Even at the moment of what seemed like her greatest defeat, she had taken care to make certain she looked every inch a queen. She wore a mantle of purple silk, earrings made of lapis lazuli, and a diadem that adorned her dark curls, marking her Greek royal lineage.

She would not allow this Octavian to defeat

her. With her children and her plan in place, victory could still be hers.

Determination flowed through her veins, and she stepped out of her chamber to face her enemy.

CHAPTER 1

Present Day
Rome, Italy
8:16 P.M.

Sebastian Rossi inhaled the brisk spring night air as he strolled down the cobble-stoned streets of the Trastevere neighborhood, a smile tugging at the corner of his lips.

He was still buzzing with adrenaline after delivering a lecture on the various languages spoken in Ptolemaic Egypt, one of many lectures held during the annual Languages of Antiquity conference. It was a lecture he had given many times back in the States, and it was one of his most popular ones, covering the languages spoken in Cleopatra's Egypt, from the Greek of the royal quarter to the Egyptian spoken by the natives. Given that one of his academic specialties was the

Ptolemaic royal family, he'd fielded many questions afterward about the most famous Ptolemy's command of multiple languages . . . Cleopatra.

The interest in Cleopatra had grown in recent weeks due to a recent explosive archaeological find —and then theft—in Rome. A team of archaeologists had found a cadre of hidden items believed to belong to a wealthy Greco-Roman woman during renovations of an old home near the Palpatine Hill.

The artifacts weren't just any artifacts, and the woman not just any wealthy woman.

EXPLOSIVE FIND IN ROME!

LINK TO CLEOPATRA DISCOVERED IN ROME

IS CLEOPATRA'S TOMB NEXT?

Those were just some of the headlines spouted from the top news organizations all over the world, because the artifacts were believed to belong to Cleopatra's daughter, a little-known historical figure compared to her famous mother. Many didn't know that Cleopatra's daughter lived to adulthood, though she eventually died during childbirth after spending her formative years in Rome with the family of the man who defeated her mother, Emperor Augustus.

Based on several artifacts linked to Cleopatra, mainly an amethyst signet ring written about in antiquity, other items of jewelry found were believed to come from Egypt, specifically the royal quarter of Alexandria. Historians had determined that the jewelry likely belonged to Cleopatra's daughter during her years spent in Rome.

Their theft had turned an already explosive find into a highly publicized mystery. The theft had occurred just one week ago. Given his area of expertise, Sebastian had reached out to the Art Crimes division of the FBI, who were helping the local Italian authorities, along with other law enforcement agencies from all over the world, which wasn't surprising given how high profile the theft was. Sebastian had offered his expertise should they need it, but they had politely turned him down.

He'd not told them his fear that there may be another motive behind the theft.

Icy fear crawled down his spine at the thought. He'd only told two other people his theory, and he trusted them. Ever since the theft, he'd told himself the thieves were just after the artifacts for their value, which was in the range of hundreds of millions of dollars.

But doubt niggled at him. Did someone else know what they could yield?

None of that is your concern, he told himself. The authorities were working on locating the artifacts; he just had to pray they were found before they got into the wrong hands. *If they weren't already.*

Forcing the unpleasant thoughts aside, he turned onto the bustling Viale Trastevere, making his way toward his hotel. The conference organizers had offered him a car to take home from the conference, which was held at the American University of Rome, but he'd opted to walk instead, wanting to enjoy the streets of Rome at night.

It was one of those perfect late spring evenings, with the city buzzing around him, the lights of Rome highlighting the modern and ancient buildings alike. Rome in the spring was his wife Mira's favorite, and he felt a pang, wishing that both Mira and their seventeen-year-old daughter, Celeste, were here with him.

They were currently in Milan, where Celeste wanted to do some shopping, and Mira, an art enthusiast, wanted to take in some of the galleries there. Just before his lecture, Mira had texted him a photo of her and Celeste. They were making faces at the camera, their joy infectious.

He smiled at the memory. It was good to see them so close after a tense few weeks. Celeste wanted to go to college in California, something Mira had ardently opposed as it was far from their Upper West Side Manhattan home. Their home had been a bastion of tension during the past few weeks, until he'd suggested they take a side trip to Milan for shopping and sightseeing while he attended the conference in Rome, hoping it would force them to reconcile. It looked like his plan had worked.

Sebastian stopped abruptly, the hairs on the back of his neck prickling with sudden awareness.

Someone was watching him.

He turned, his gaze sweeping over the various passersby, but no one paid him any mind. He shook off the sensation and continued on until he reached his hotel, though he kept up a periodic scan of his surroundings.

"Doctor Rossi," the hotel's doorman, a friendly Italian by the name of Lorenzo, who knew him from his previous stays, greeted him with a wide smile. "How was the lecture?"

"It went well," Sebastian replied. "I didn't put too many people to sleep."

Lorenzo chuckled as Sebastian gave him a wry grin, heading toward the elevator.

When Sebastian entered his dark, spacious hotel room, he decided that tonight he'd enjoy a nice glass of red wine on the balcony, a Sangiovese. His wine drinking was a tradition of sorts, a treat he gave himself after delivering a guest lecture or finishing an exhaustive piece of research.

Placing down his bag, he entered the small kitchenette, flipping on the light. He beamed at the sight of a brand-new bottle of Sangiovese with a note stuck to its front on the counter. He peeled it off.

Best of luck tonight. Love, Mira and Celeste.

He smiled down at the note, his heart swelling with love. His Mira knew all about his ritual and must have had the bottle sent over. Still smiling, he decided to place a FaceTime call to his girls before his celebratory drink.

But as he turned to exit the kitchenette, he froze, spotting a movement out of the corner of his eye.

In the other room, a shadow had *moved.*

Heart hammering, he stood still for a moment, wondering if his eyes were playing tricks on him. His mouth dry, he took a cautious step forward and flipped on the light.

Light flooded the room, and he scanned the corner where he'd seen the movement. There was nothing there other than a bookcase and a tall plant.

He shook his head, silently scolding himself. First that sensation of someone watching him while he'd walked, and now this. Maybe he needed to start on that wine now.

He turned to head back to the kitchenette, but he halted. He heard something, and this time he was certain he hadn't imagined it.

Several steady footsteps, and a loud click that seemed to echo off the walls. The light that had flooded the room went out, and a tidal wave of panic swept over Sebastian.

Flee, his mind screamed. *Get out. Now.*

But as he whirled, on the verge of racing toward the door, a tall figure emerged from the shadows, and a heavily accented voice murmured, "I wouldn't do that, Doctor Rossi."

Sebastian cried out as a blinding pain throbbed behind his temples. The intruder had struck him from behind.

As Sebastian's world went entirely black, he thought, with a swirling sense of dread . . .

Someone knows.

CHAPTER 2

Rome, Italy
2:15 A.M.

As Adrian's cell phone buzzed on the nightstand, penetrating her haze of sleep, she assumed it was her mother again.

She'd steadfastly ignored her mother's calls for the past two days. She didn't need to listen to the voice mails to know what the calls were about. It was the same call she got every year around this time. *As if I could ever forget what happened on this day ten years ago.*

The day that had changed her life forever.

She kept her eyes closed, determined to ignore it and get back to sleep, but almost as soon as the cell stopped buzzing, it started up again.

Heaving a sigh, she sat up, reaching for her phone, and froze when she saw who it was.

Though she hadn't spoken to her former FBI

partner in years, she still had his number programmed into her phone. Nick Harper.

Why would he be calling her in the middle of the night? She swallowed, unease gripping her as she answered the call.

"Adrian. It's me."

His voice was exactly as she remembered, a calming, deep baritone. When they were partners, he'd used that voice on suspects to lure them into a sense of ease before springing the trap. She used to joke that he had the voice of a hypnotherapist.

"I'm sorry to call you in the middle of the night, but I think you'd want to know about this." There was a long pause before he continued. "It's Sebastian Rossi. He's gone missing from his hotel room."

It took several moments for his words to pierce the fog of her still sleep-addled brain. But once it did, fear bloomed in her chest, along with dread, as dark memories pulled her to the past.

Another phone ringing in the middle of the night. Her mother answering the call, her face draining of color.

Not again, she thought, panic gripping her gut. *Not Sebastian.*

Sebastian Rossi was like a father to her. He'd been her professor during her graduate studies in ancient languages at Columbia University, becoming a trusted mentor and advisor, and they'd remained in contact long after she graduated and became a consulting lecturer and professor of ancient languages and manuscripts at New York

University. She'd even become close with his wife, Mira and their daughter, Celeste. Mira jokingly— and lovingly—referred to Adrian as their bonus adult daughter.

She and Sebastian were both in Rome for the same conference; she'd sent him an email this morning from the airport wishing him luck at his lecture tonight, something she would have attended, but her flight had arrived after his lecture.

"What happened?" Adrian demanded, stumbling out of bed.

"A guest in the hotel room next to his heard signs of a struggle and called the front desk. Security found blood on the floor and Sebastian missing."

Panic seared her veins; she hurriedly got dressed as she put the call on speaker. "Why are you there? Isn't this something the local police would handle?"

"The detective on duty called me when they found my contact info among his things. He thought that whatever the FBI was talking to him about may be a reason he was taken—if he was taken."

"Why was Sebastian talking to the FBI?"

There was a long pause. "You really should get here, Adrian."

"I'll be there as soon as I can."

It didn't take long to get ready, even though she was rattled. *Amazing what sheer panic will do*, she thought wryly. She tugged her long dark waves back into a messy bun before grabbing her bag and hurrying down to the lobby, where she had the concerned-looking receptionist, no doubt seeing the panic in her eyes, call for a cab.

As the cab made its way through the streets of the Trastevere neighborhood toward Sebastian's hotel, frantic thoughts raced through her mind. Had someone abducted Sebastian? Who would want to do such a thing? He was extremely well-liked by his students and other professors alike. He was probably the smartest person she knew, yet he was never condescending, only open and kind with his knowledge.

Her throat clenched as she thought of Mira and Celeste. They were such a close-knit family; they would be devastated if—

Not going there. She wouldn't let herself finish that thought. Maybe he'd simply injured himself and left to get medical attention. She tried to imagine Sebastian walking into his hotel room at any moment, annoyed at the presence of police.

But her gut instinct, one that had served her well during her days as a criminal profiler for the FBI, told her this wasn't the case. Sebastian wouldn't just take off without a trace.

Something was terribly wrong.

2:37 *A.M.*

AFTER THE CAB dropped her off at Sebastian's hotel, she identified herself to the harried young officers who stood in the lobby, one of whom led her up to Sebastian's room.

She spotted Nick immediately among the Italian authorities. He was as boyishly handsome as she remembered, tall and fit, with warm blue eyes and dark hair.

Nick approached, offering her a small smile before reaching out to give her a firm embrace. She returned it, and a distant emotion stirred in her, bringing up memories of the past. But she firmly pushed the feeling aside. Now was not the time.

"It's good to see you, West," Nick said, resorting to his old habit of calling her by her last name. She couldn't help the smile that tugged at her lips, one which dissipated as she took in the hotel room, which appeared orderly.

"His bags are gone, along with his cell phone," Nick said, following her gaze.

"The hotel security cameras?"

"Conveniently not working on this floor. The police are talking to security and interviewing hotel guests. But other than the guest who heard the noise and reported it to the front desk, no one reported seeing anyone or anything suspicious. I'm going to reach out to attendees at a lecture he gave earlier tonight."

Adrian nodded, considering this. "What were you talking to Sebastian about?"

"He reached out to us about the theft of the

Cleopatra artifacts, offering his expertise should we need it. I told him we have all the expertise we need, we just want leads." Regret flickered across his face.

Unease crept down Adrian's spine. She had heard of the theft; you had to be living under a rock not to. She and Sebastian had exchanged emails when they were initially discovered; his excitement was palpable in his messages, and when they were stolen, he was devastated. Could Sebastian have somehow gotten entangled with the theft of the artifacts? Is that why someone had abducted him?

"Do you think there's a link? If he was asking about the stolen artifacts—"

"I don't know," Nick said, heaving a sigh. "We have no leads on the artifacts. And if he was taken because of them—why? What use would the thieves have for him when they already have the artifacts?" He met her eyes, his brows knitted together in a frown. "Do you know if he was working on any special projects? Something that would make someone want to harm him?"

Adrian crawled through her memories, recalling one in particular. "He told me a couple of weeks ago that he was working on a secret project . . . he wouldn't tell me anything about it. I thought nothing of it at the time because Sebastian is always working on a secret project."

Now Adrian wanted to kick herself for not paying more attention to the hints Sebastian had dropped about the secret project he was working on. *This could be explosive, Adrian,* he'd said. But Sebastian was infinitely curious and always doing research on some theory, usually revolving around an ancient language that fascinated him.

An Italian officer approached and pulled Nick away; he gave her an apologetic smile and trailed him. Adrian looked around the room, unable to stop her criminal profiler brain from working.

Nothing else seemed to have been taken or was out of order. Given how Sebastian's abduction had occurred, whoever did this was highly efficient and had likely done this before. A professional. Possibly a contract job, something typically done in the underworld or organized crime.

But Adrian had known Sebastian for a long time. He was squeaky clean, without so much as a parking ticket to his name. How would such an individual even know about Sebastian? She thought of the theft of the Cleopatra artifacts, the "secret project" Sebastian was working on. *No such thing as coincidence.*

"Sorry about that. Paperwork to be signed," Nick said, returning. He paused, giving her a grin. "I know you can't help yourself. You can take the woman out of the FBI, but not the FBI out of the woman. What are you thinking?"

"That whoever took him is a professional. Look how clean this crime scene is. And no one saw anything. The question is—why?"

"Exactly," Nick said, raking his hand through his dark hair, something he did whenever something flummoxed him. "I'm going to head to the office he was using here in Rome to see what else I can dig up." He studied her for a long moment. "Do you want to come?"

Adrian hesitated, but only for a moment. She had chosen to leave the FBI and the world of criminal investigation behind, but this was different. This was Sebastian. She wouldn't be able to rest until she knew he was safe.

"Let's go," she said, already walking out ahead of him.

CHAPTER 3

Rome, Italy
2:45 A.M.

"Has the professor been taken care of?" Yara Elmasry asked, her cell phone pressed to her ear, as her driver wound his way through the streets of Centro Storico.

"Yes, my brother handled it as you requested. And he's secured, my *kukla*," Leonid replied.

Yara inwardly flinched at his term of endearment for her. The Russian word for "doll." Though they were lovers, Leonid only served a means to an end; he and his brother, Markos, had come highly recommended from one of her contacts. *Efficient and brutal*, they'd described both him and Markos. All she'd known about them was that they both had a military background and had briefly worked in foreign intelligence before becoming mercenaries who worked for some of the top names in the underworld.

When Yara had met them for the first time, she'd seen the lust in Leonid's eyes and hid away her disgust to use his attraction to her advantage. His brother, Markos, however, had been all business, focused on the task at hand. She trusted him more to carry out the successful abduction of the professor. She had sensed that Leonid was more impulsive and needed to be kept on a tighter leash.

Men are weak; their lust rules them, Dalal, her beloved friend and mentor, had once told her, when she was younger and so very broken. *Use it to your advantage. Always.*

She had once asked Dalal why their organization, an organization led by women for the betterment of women worldwide, employed men. Dalal had merely smiled and told her that men still had their uses, especially when it came to brute force and violence, something that the organization would need to obtain its goals.

"Good. I'm just returning from a late dinner. I'll be there shortly," Yara said to Leonid now. She lowered her voice, making certain it had taken on a seductive air, as she murmured, "I will see you soon, my volk."

On the other end of the line, she could hear Leonid's breath quicken, and she had to stop herself from rolling her eyes. Like most men who only thought with their southern regions, he was far too easy to deceive.

As she hung up, she felt the concerned eyes of Fairuza, her young colleague, trained on her. When Yara met her gaze, she flushed and looked away.

"What is it, Fairuza?"

"How can we be certain Sebastian Rossi will find what we're looking for? Several of our people looked over the artifacts and could find nothing."

"If there is something to be found—and I'm certain there is—Doctor Rossi is the one to find it," she said.

Fairuza nodded, but she still looked uncertain. Yara could forgive her for her uncertainty. She had once been like Fairuza, innocent and docile.

Fairuza was a college student recruited by another member. Her family had disowned her for running away from an arranged marriage to a man thirty years her senior; she'd moved in with an aunt who lived in London. Yara had taken the younger woman under her wing, and Fairuza was almost as close to her as her own mentor, Dalal, had been.

Grief coursed through Yara at the thought of Dalal, who had died after a long battle with cancer the year before. It was because of her that Yara's life had changed for the better. Dalal had taken her from the broken young woman she'd been to the determined leader of the secret organization that Dalal herself had once spearheaded. *I won't let you down, Dalal,* Yara silently promised.

When she'd learned of the discovery of the Cleopatra artifacts, she'd arranged for their theft, which had been surprisingly easy. She'd underestimated how bribable low-paid security guards and even museum employees were.

It wasn't the artifacts themselves that were her endgame; it was what they could lead to, something she knew about, thanks to Doctor Rossi. And that could change everything for her, her organization . . . and the world.

She took out her phone, opening the secret folder that contained photos of the artifacts. She ran her fingers over the images, thinking of the immense change they would bring.

It would be the beginning of a new world order.

American University of Rome
Rome, Italy
2:50 A.M.

THE AMERICAN UNIVERSITY OF ROME sat perched on the precipice of the ancient Janiculum Hill, one of the tallest hills in Rome. It was named for the Roman god Janus, god of gates and transitions, from whom the month of January derives its name. Since antiquity, it offered stunning views of the surrounding city; priests would observe the behavior of birds from this hill, using their behavior as omens.

The campus itself was dotted with two lush gardens, with many of its buildings located along the Aurelian Walls, which were ancient walls of the city.

Adrian trailed Nick along the path of the old walls until they reached Sebastian's building, heading up the stairs and making their way down a long corridor until they reached Sebastian's temp office, which was unlocked.

Adrian's gaze swept over the office as they entered, a lump forming in her throat. It was as messy as his office back at Columbia, with scattered papers and folders on every surface and haphazardly piled stacks of books. She'd often teased Sebastian that his office perpetually looked as if a tornado had struck it.

Her thoughts returned to the excitement in Sebastian's voice when they'd last spoken, as he'd told her about the secret project he was working on. *This could be explosive, Adrian,* he'd said, but refused to give her any further information, insisting what he was working on wasn't yet complete.

What did you find, Sebastian? she wondered now. *And what was it about your discovery that would make someone abduct you?*

Nick was moving around the office, his gloved hands working with efficiency as he looked through the neatly stacked folders and documents on Sebastian's desk. Adrian looked around, her eyes landing on the familiar analog calendar Sebastian took everywhere with him. He refused to use the calendar on his phone or laptop, insisting that he didn't trust any historian who didn't use at least one "old-fashioned" item.

She moved over to it and ran her finger down the entry list, going still as she saw Sebastian was scheduled to meet with Professor Roberta Fields the next day.

!!Urgent meeting with Roberta!! Talk with her ASAP

Adrian stilled. She knew Professor Fields; she'd been an adjunct professor at Columbia when Adrian was still a student there. Fields was an expert on ancient Rome and Ptolemaic Egypt. Could Sebastian have shared his mysterious discovery with her?

"Nick," she said. "Come take a look at this."

Nick approached, leaning in to study the calendar. Adrian met his eyes, her heart hammering. It was the middle of the night, but if Roberta knew what could have made Sebastian a target, they needed to see her—now.

Nick seemed to read her mind.

"Let's go pay Professor Fields a visit."

CHAPTER 4

Unknown
3:02 A.M.

Sebastian came to with a gasp.

He looked around; complete and total darkness surrounded him. His hands were bound behind him, and he sat on a cold stone floor. For a moment, he had no idea how he'd gotten here.

And then the memories slammed into him.

Returning to his hotel from the conference. The shadow that moved. A man's low, threatening voice. The stab of pain behind his temples.

His head still ached, and now panic swelled. He took a deep, shuddering breath to calm himself. Where was he? Who had taken him? He stretched his bound hands out in front of him until his hands grasped what felt like a concrete wall. He stumbled to his feet, relieved that his feet weren't bound, feeling along the walls, hoping to eventually feel a door.

But the concrete remained steady, and he wondered in horror if he was being held in some cement-style box.

"Help!" he cried out, though he knew it was likely fruitless. He heard no sound anywhere, no sign of life. It was as if he were being held in a dark void. "Please!"

Silence was his only answer. Sebastian sank back against the wall, his pulse thrumming. He needed to calm himself, to think rationally, to stick only to the facts.

Someone had abducted him from his hotel room. He was still alive, which indicated his abductor needed him alive . . . for now. Why would anyone want to abduct him?

Even as he asked himself the question, he knew the answer. He knew down to the marrow of his bones, as much as he wanted to deny it to himself. *I thought I'd been so careful.*

The sound of grinding tore into his thoughts, and it took several moments for him to realize it was the sound of a door being pushed open. A brief shaft of light shone in the room as a male figure entered, closing the door with another grinding creak.

Sebastian stumbled back on instinct, holding his bound hands in front of him in a protective gesture. He was a fifty-five-year-old professor, hardly in the type of shape to ward off a physical attack, but he would do whatever necessary to protect himself.

"What—what do you want?" Sebastian demanded. "Who are you? Why am I here?"

The man didn't answer, but Sebastian could hear his steady breathing as he approached. Sebastian took another faltering step back, stumbling over his own feet and crashing to the ground, his back hitting the wall hard.

Still, the man continued his leisurely approach, crouching down before him. He held something up, and Sebastian jerked back, fearing that it was a gun, but he realized it was an iPad.

Shaking, he watched as the tablet lit up, displaying a video. Sebastian watched with growing horror as he saw that the video was of his wife and daughter. They were in their hotel room, removing items from shopping bags and chattering, clearly oblivious to the fact that they were being filmed.

Anger overtook his fear, and Sebastian lunged toward the man, but a solid fist in his face had him rearing back, his head landing hard on the floor. He felt the warm trickle of blood on his face.

When the man spoke, it was in heavily accented English.

"You will not make any moves toward me again or I will see to it that they are harmed," he said, his voice ice cold. "Do you understand?"

Terror coursing through him, Sebastian nodded his head. The man turned the tablet around, tapped on something, then turned it back toward Sebastian.

This time, the images on the screen were of photos. He recognized them; websites and newspapers all around the world had splashed them all over their front pages.

The stolen Cleopatra artifacts.

"You know what we are looking for."

Sebastian swallowed hard, trying to feign ignorance. "No. I don't know—"

A stinging pain hit his cheek and Sebastian realized his abductor had struck him again. His face throbbed with pain.

"You know what we are looking for," the man repeated.

"I don't know what you're talking about. Please—"

The man lowered the tablet, taking a cell phone out of his pocket. He stood, dialing a number. "You have my permission to approach the wife and daughter."

"No! No, please. OK. OK, yes, I know what you're looking for. I know!" Sebastian cried, panic seizing him. *Please don't let any harm come to Mira and Celeste,* he prayed. *Please.*

There was a long pause, and in the darkness, he could barely make out the man considering him.

"Never mind," his abductor said into the phone, after a long pause. "But remain on standby."

He stepped forward. Sebastian shrank back, but the man merely dropped the tablet into his lap.

He moved to the door, and Sebastian thought he was leaving him, but light suddenly flooded the room, so bright that it nearly blinded Sebastian. He had to blink his eyes to adjust.

The room he was in was small and windowless, with concrete walls and a stone floor. It looked like a jail cell. The man who stood by the door was massively tall, broad-shouldered and muscular; Sebastian knew that even if he were younger and fitter, he wouldn't be able to win a physical fight with this man.

"You have twenty-four hours to tell us what we want to know," his abductor said, turning to exit, leaving a terrified Sebastian in his wake.

CHAPTER 5

Rome, Italy
3:07 A.M.

*R*oberta's home wasn't far from the American University of Rome, tucked away on a small residential street at the edge of the Travastere neighborhood. Adrian hung back to let Nick knock, praying that she was home and awake.

The door swung open after only several sharp raps on the door.

Roberta Fields was in her late fifties, with gray streaked auburn hair and brown eyes that shone with intelligence. She looked much older to Adrian since she'd last seen her at another conference two years prior; there was a wariness to her that hadn't been there before. *She's just tired,* Adrian scolded herself. *It's the middle of the night. You probably woke her up.*

Roberta blinked in surprise. "Adrian."

"I know it's late," Adrian said, giving her an apologetic look. "But there's been an emergency with Sebastian. This is Agent Nick Harper, he's with the FBI. We need to talk to you."

The color drained from Roberta's face, and she took a faltering step back.

"S-Sebastian?" she stammered. "What happened?"

~

MOMENTS LATER, Adrian and Nick sat opposite Roberta in her spacious living room. Adrian had told her about the circumstances around Sebastian's disappearance, and her face had grown increasingly pale.

"Sebastian agreed to do a joint lecture with me later this week for the conference, but I hadn't heard from him about his part of the presentation. That's why it was urgent that we meet," she said.

Adrian noticed she wasn't looking at them as she spoke, a classic avoidance move. *She's hiding something.*

"Was there anything in particular he was working on? Anything he discussed with you that might put him in someone's crosshairs?" Adrian asked.

"All we talked about the last couple of weeks were the upcoming lectures for the conference, and he gave me advice for the syllabus of my classes for the upcoming semester."

This time Roberta looked at them, and Adrian searched her eyes. She was harder to read this time, but she still sensed that she was hiding something.

But what? If this were a suspect, Adrian would draw this out, using every psychological trick in the book to get her to tell them the truth. Yet there was no time for such a thing. The longer Sebastian was missing, the more danger he was in.

She turned to Nick. "Can you give me and Professor Fields a moment alone?"

Nick frowned, looking puzzled, but at the insistent look in her eyes he acquiesced. He stood, giving them both a polite nod before leaving.

Adrian waited until Nick had closed the front door behind him before speaking.

"Roberta," she said, leaning forward and giving her an imploring look. "If there's anything you know that can help, anything at all, it can help Sebastian. This is me asking, OK? Not the FBI. I'm afraid he may be in danger."

Roberta met her eyes. Something unreadable flared in the depths of her own before it vanished, and she looked away.

"I wish I did," she said stiffly, getting to her feet. "It's late. If I think of anything, I'll contact you."

Adrian wanted to press her, to find out what she was hiding, but she knew it would do no good. She could tell by the shuttered expression on Roberta's face that she wasn't going to open up.

Adrian stood, trying to make eye contact with Roberta, but she determinedly avoided her gaze. "If you change your mind, you know how to reach me," Adrian said. "And if you know anything—"

"I don't," Roberta said shortly. She moved to the front door and opened it, still not looking at Adrian.

A clear dismissal.

"She's lying," Adrian said when she reached Nick, who was leaning against his car, moments later.

"Agreed," Nick said grimly.

Adrian glanced back at Roberta's home. She didn't know her as well as she knew Sebastian, but she hardly seemed the type to be involved in an abduction.

But if she was involved, what was the motive?

"There's that mind again, at work," Nick observed, grinning as they slid into the car.

"If she's involved, I'm trying to figure out why—and how."

"Only one way to find out. We find out as much as we can about her, see what dead bodies we can dig up," Nick said. "Then we go back to her with what we know, pressure her to open up."

Adrian nodded, though nervousness flared in her gut. A full background check would take time, but she didn't have any other ideas. *And*, she reminded herself, *you're no longer an FBI agent. You have no real say in how Nick carries out his investigation.*

She could only hope they had enough time to get to Sebastian—wherever he was.

LEONID WATCHED THE TALL, dark-haired man and the willowy, attractive woman leave Roberta Fields' house, his eyebrows knitted together in a frown.

Yara wanted him to keep an eye on Fields, especially after word got out about Sebastian's disappearance; she wanted to make certain that she kept quiet.

Leonid had thought Yara was being unnecessarily paranoid; Fields would be dead in an instant if she dared speak to the authorities, and the woman was a coward.

But now, he wasn't so certain. The man and woman leaving both had the look of law enforcement officials, though they wore no uniforms. He'd seen and interacted with enough such people to know the typical look and how they carried themselves.

He watched as they entered the man's car and drove off, his gaze returning to Fields' home. *What are you doing talking to law enforcement officials in the middle of the night, Professor Fields?*

He picked up his cell and dialed Yara's number.

"Yara," he said, and told her about Fields' late-night visitors.

There was a long pause; he could practically taste Yara's fury on the other end of the line. In spite of himself, arousal stirred in his groin. Yara was even sexier when she was angry.

It was his first time working for a woman. He'd almost not taken the job but had chosen to do so at his brother Markos' insistence. Jobs were coming fewer in between.

He scowled as he thought of his brother. He and Markos usually worked in tandem, yet Yara had entrusted him to take on the abduction. Jealousy had coursed through him at the trust she'd given Markos. He knew his brother had the tendency to be more focused—even more ruthless than he was—so it was probably the wisest choice. Still, it bruised his ego. Like Markos, he'd been a top mercenary soldier, a spy prized in the intelligence sector, and Yara was treating him like a glorified babysitter.

"Do you think she talked?" Yara asked.

"I don't know," he said honestly, stamping down his irritation. "They weren't in there long, and they didn't look so happy when they left."

Another long pause.

"This is what I want you to do."

Despite his irritation with her, he could recall how he'd felt when he'd first seen her and taken in her dark, alluring beauty. It had been lust at first sight. Markos had scolded him for thinking with his nether regions, and yes, he was guilty of that, even now. But what turned him on the most about Yara was her ruthlessness.

As he listened to her orders now, he smiled.

His *kukla* was ruthless indeed.

CHAPTER 6

Embassy of the United States - FBI Offices
Rome, Italy
4:15 A.M.

The Federal Bureau of Investigation's office in Rome, officially called the legal attaché office, was located in the American Embassy, nestled in the Palazzo Margherita.

The bureau's office was tucked away in its own section, and despite being in another country and mostly empty at this hour, Adrian felt like she had returned to the office she'd worked in back in DC. With Nick at her side, it seemed disconcertingly like she'd never left, and that her years in academia, of trying to build a normal life, hadn't happened at all.

She could recall the times she'd enjoyed. Early morning coffee runs with Nick, brainstorming over cases in her office with him and other agents, or reaching a crucial breakthrough that would crack a missing persons' or murder case.

Unfortunately, these memories came with the bad ones. Her growing frustration with the bureau's bureaucracy, departmental turf wars that prevented necessary work from being done, and her increasing conflicts with her superiors.

And then that final, awful case which had made her decide to leave law enforcement for good.

"Sebastian offers his help to locate the artifacts," Nick said, glancing over at her. He was walking briskly at her side, his brow furrowed, looking deep in thought. "And he's also working on a secret project—something he tells me is explosive. Maybe he tells Roberta Fields about what he's working on. And now, Roberta Fields is hiding something."

This was something they'd done back during their days as partners. Whenever there was a baffling case or something they had difficulty figuring out, they would spitball the facts of the case out loud. They'd easily—and quickly—fallen back into their old routine.

"It's all linked. It has to be," she said.

"Agreed," Nick said. "I want to introduce you to someone who can help us possibly untangle all this."

He led her to a sectioned-off area of the offices, filled to the brim with bays of computers. He made a beeline toward the lone young man who was working at this hour; he sat in front of his own personal bay of three monitors, large headphones perched on his ears, bopping along to music only he could hear. Nick tapped his shoulder and the young man started, reaching up to slide off his headphones.

"What do you want, Harper?" he grumbled, though his dark eyes twinkled with mischief. "I was in the middle of my favorite song."

"You can get back to goofing off and pretending to work in a second. I want to introduce you to someone, and then I need your help with something," Nick said, giving him a playful scowl. "Vince, this is Adrian West. Adrian, this is Vince, our—and please don't get a big head about this, Vince—our tech whiz."

Vince took off his headphones and stood, extending his hand to Adrian. He was tall and lanky, and looked more like a member of a punk rock band than a tech for the bureau, with strategically spiked dark hair and colorful tattoos peeking out beneath the collar of his white button-down shirt. She wondered what someone who looked so anti-establishment was doing working in federal law enforcement.

Vince shook her hand. "Nice to meet you. I've heard a lot of things about you from this guy. Mostly him trying to take credit for all the cases *you* probably solved when you were partners."

Adrian returned his grin, liking him already. "I'm not surprised."

"Ha ha," Nick said warily, before turning back

to face Vince, his expression turning serious. "We need a full background check on a woman named Roberta Fields. Let me know what you can dig up ASAP, she may have info on a missing person."

As they left Vince, who gave them a dutiful nod, Nick said, "I also have to talk to Sebastian's wife. We've notified her about Sebastian, but I need to see if she has any insight into what he was working on."

Adrian stilled at the mention of Mira. *Damn it.* She should have called her immediately.

"Is she here?" she asked.

"She and their daughter are on their way from Milan now."

"Let me talk to her," Adrian said. "I know her; it will be easier if she talks to me."

Nick nodded. "OK. I have to file a report and talk to my boss. You can call Mira from my office. Take a nap if you need to, this might take a while. You remember FBI bureaucracy," he added, giving her a crooked smile. Adrian returned his smile, but it was tight. She did . . . all too well.

He opened the door and ushered Adrian inside. Nick's office was small and cluttered, almost as messy as Sebastian's. She couldn't help but smile when she saw the familiar poster on the wall, the same one that had hung in Nick's office back in DC. *I'm an FBI Agent. Red Tape is my middle name.*

"I see you still have the poster."

"Of course. It's my signature," Nick said,

returning her grin. He studied her for a long moment before continuing, "I wish the circumstances were different, but it's good to be working with you again, Adrian."

He reached out to place his hand over hers, causing warmth to flare beneath her skin. Though worry still filled her, his words put her at ease. She'd forgotten how comfortable she'd always felt in his presence . . . how right it felt.

Their relationship had never been romantic in the past; Nick was dating a fellow agent when they'd first started working together. And though Adrian had always found him attractive, she'd decided early on that it was never a good idea to let the lines between work, friendship, and romantic relationship cross.

Yet toward the end of their partnership, a subtle shift had occurred between them during the final case they'd worked on together. It was a closeness that went beyond friendship, and they'd come perilously close to a kiss. Adrian had been the one to pull back before it could happen, and they'd never spoken of the moment again. It wasn't long after this that Adrian had resigned and left the bureau—and their intensifying relationship —behind.

A stab of guilt pierced her; she'd known that Nick was hurt when she'd chosen to leave, and he had exhibited no bitterness, but she'd always regretted the way she left things.

"Nick, I know I never actually apologized for—for the way I left things— "

"Hey," Nick interrupted, shaking his head. "It's all in the past. I only wept a little bit."

He cracked a smile, and Adrian returned it. "As long as it was only a little bit." She studied him a moment. "Why did you switch from Violent Crimes to Art Crimes?"

Nick's smile faded, a shadow passing over his face. "I think I just got tired of chasing . . . death. It got to me after a while, especially once you left."

Their gazes held for another beat, a moment of shared understanding passing between them, before Nick turned to leave.

Adrian watched him go before settling onto a lumpy couch tucked into the corner of the office and took a deep breath before dialing Mira. Mira answered on the first ring.

"Adrian," Mira said, her voice tight with worry. "We're on our way to Rome now. Please tell me it isn't true."

"I wish I could," Adrian said with a sigh.

"I don't understand. Who would want to harm Sebastian? Maybe—maybe it's some type of misunderstanding?"

The fragile hope in Mira's voice tugged at her. She wanted to tell her that Sebastian would be fine, but she couldn't. Hadn't she herself been in this position once? In her case, it hadn't turned out to be fine. She swallowed, pushing past the painful memory.

"The authorities are doing everything they can to find him."

"Are you helping them?" Mira asked, sounding hopeful.

"I'll do what I can, but I'm not a federal agent anymore. My former partner is on the case. He's the one who called me to let me know what's happening."

"I know I have no right to ask you this, but please stay on the investigation. Sebastian told me what a good investigator you were before you left the FBI. I know how much you care about him. Knowing that someone who cares about him is looking will put me at ease."

Adrian closed her eyes. She hadn't exactly left the FBI on good terms, but neither Mira nor Sebastian knew the story around that. Anxiety filled her at the subtle promise Mira was asking her to make.

"I'll keep looking, whether or not they keep me on," she said finally. There was really no other choice. She'd have no peace until she knew Sebastian was all right, especially now that there was growing evidence of the danger he was in. "Mira, do you know what Sebastian was working on? He mentioned a secret project to me."

"No," Mira said, her tone heavy with regret. "But you know Sebastian; he's always working on some side project. I can look through his things to see if I can find anything of note."

"Thanks," Adrian said, as her mind seized on another possibility. "Were there any burglaries at your apartment or Sebastian's office at Columbia recently?"

"No," Mira said, sounding alarmed. "Why?"

Adrian didn't want to frighten Mira, but she needed to know how far back this was planned and if Sebastian's abductor or abductors had international ties. It could help piece together a timeline.

"If his abduction was caused by something he's working on, it would make sense that your apartment or his office were searched. Is there someone in New York who can check in on your apartment?"

"Yes, my sister," Mira said. Pain filled her voice, and Adrian regretted causing it, but this information could help find Sebastian. "I'll check and let you know."

There was a long, fraught silence on the other end of the line, and Adrian made herself speak, delivering a promise she prayed she could keep.

"We'll find him, Mira."

CHAPTER 7

Unknown
4:21 A.M.

Sebastian tried to concentrate on the images before him, but terror had taken hold. All he could think of was his wife and daughter, and the danger they were in.

He could only pray that law enforcement was looking for him, and had his family on their radar. He thought of the encrypted message he kept buried in his notes, something he'd thought he was being overly paranoid about creating.

It seemed he wasn't so paranoid after all.

One of the few people who would know how to decode it was Adrian West, his brilliant former student turned bonus daughter and close friend. She was in Rome for the conference, and as a close friend and colleague of his, the authorities would likely—he prayed—reach out to her once his disappearance was noticed. If she could find his message, there was hope.

But if no one realized he was gone in time, and his abductor got to Mira and Celeste—

Focus, he scolded himself, returning his gaze to the images on the tablet before him. He couldn't let his thoughts chase such a horrifying outcome.

Under any other circumstances, awe would have filled him at the sight of the precious artifacts before him. Jewels worn by the most famous woman of antiquity.

The artifacts consisted of several items of jewelry. A pair of exquisite gold, pearl and lapis lazuli earrings in the shape of Egyptian crowns. Two pendants, one with an image of a Ptolemaic queen who was most likely Cleopatra herself.

But the two most prized finds were the second pendant, featuring the image of a young queen wearing the diadem of Ptolemaic royalty, with the inscription of Cleopatra Selene, the name of Cleopatra's daughter. The other was a well-preserved amethyst ring, referenced in antiquity as being worn by Cleopatra herself.

There was no mistaking the finery or the craftsmanship of the jewels, even after centuries had gone by. He could just imagine the earrings gracing Cleopatra's ears, the pendant dangling from a necklace around her neck. Did Julius Caesar or Mark Antony marvel over their beauty? Had they handled the jewelry themselves?

Given the materials and style, archaeologists

had instantly been able to tell that the jewelry was not akin to the type of jewelry worn by Roman women at the time. The pendant with Cleopatra Selene's name inscribed and the famous amethyst ring, along with the dating of the artifacts to the time Cleopatra Selene lived in Rome after her mother's death, had all but sealed the artifacts as belonging to Cleopatra's daughter.

Yet as dazzling as the jewels were, they were merely a piece of a larger puzzle, a crucial piece of a secret theory he'd long held. It was a theory that he'd shared with only two people. He didn't want to believe that one of them had betrayed him, but how else would his abductor have known to take him?

A burning sense of betrayal seared his gut, but he ignored it. He had to believe that his abductor had found out about his theory through some other means.

As he looked at the jewels now, it was looking as if his theory was all for naught. He studied each item carefully, but for all their fine craftsmanship, they revealed no hint of any secret messages.

They were just jewels.

He closed his eyes, guilt and defeat settling over him like a great weight. He'd always known his theory was a long shot, but now that his abductors knew about it, he'd inadvertently put his life, and the lives of his wife and daughter, in danger for no reason.

He had the feeling that his abductor wouldn't

want to learn that he'd abducted Sebastian for nothing, and he sincerely doubted the man would return him to his hotel with a polite apology. No, his abductor, whoever he was, had gone through a great deal of trouble to secure both Sebastian and the artifacts.

If Sebastian couldn't give his abductor what he wanted, he was as good as dead, and Mira and Celeste . . .

Panic seized him, and he took a deep breath to quell it.

He needed to buy time. Sebastian looked up, noticing a small blinking red light embedded high in the wall. Had it been there all along? He placed down the tablet and stood, looking directly at the red light.

"If you want me to find anything," he said, hoping his voice sounded steadier than he felt, "then I need to see the artifacts myself. The photos aren't enough."

Shaking, he sat back down, his heart in his throat as he waited for some type of response.

The wait seemed to drag on for hours, with only the sound of his breathing and his thundering heartbeat competing with the raging silence. He didn't know how much time had passed until he heard footsteps, a key in the lock, and the door as it creaked open.

Sebastian was a rational man, often prone to minutes, sometimes hours, of thought before taking action. Yet at that moment, he was only thinking of survival, and not just his own. *Mira and Celeste.*

And so, he acted without thought.

He leapt to his feet and sprinted toward the opening door, but he wasn't nearly fast enough. The leg of his abductor shot out, sending him sprawling to the ground. Sebastian landed hard on his back, pain spiraling through him. His abductor stepped forward, landing solid blows to his rib cage, his back, and his face with his boot. Sebastian curled into a ball to protect his face, pain radiating throughout his body.

His captor squatted down on his haunches. Sebastian closed his eyes, not wanting to see his abductor's rage, but he could feel the heat of his breath on his skin.

Sebastian suddenly stilled, his terror a shard of ice piercing his heart when he felt the cold hardness of a gun pressed to his temple.

"Try to escape again," his abductor said roughly, "and you will watch your wife and daughter die. Slowly. I will not give you any more chances."

Sebastian nodded, his fear a physical thing bearing down on him. His abductor stood, turning back to the door.

"Wait."

Sebastian forced the word past his lips; he could barely breathe after the physical attack. His hasty attempt at escape was foolish, but he still needed to buy time.

"I-I was telling the truth," Sebastian rasped. "I need to see the artifacts in person."

There was a long silence as his abductor studied him. After several long moments, he approached Sebastian. On instinct, Sebastian shrank back as the man stepped forward, crouching down before him, his dark eyes hard and cold.

"I will bring you the artifacts. But remember my warning. I do not make empty threats."

Sebastian swallowed, offering his captor a shaky nod. There would be no more escape attempts, but he needed to provide his abductor with something.

Mira and Celeste's lives depended upon it.

CHAPTER 8

Embassy of the United States - FBI Offices
Rome, Italy
4:25 A.M.

*A*drian tried to make herself comfortable on the bulky couch in Nick's office, but her restless mind wouldn't cease buzzing. She briefly considered calling her mother but decided to hold off and send a text for now. She didn't want to tell her about Sebastian going missing or that she was joining the search. It would only worry her. Her mother had enough on her mind as it was.

She took out her phone and sent a quick text. *Hey Mom, got your message. I'm busy with the conference now but I'll call you when I can.*

Her mother responded immediately. *OK, baby. Look forward to hearing your voice.*

A stab of guilt pierced her. Adrian and her mother had never been as close as she and her father had been; their relationship had become especially strained when Adrian had joined the bureau not long after her father's disappearance a decade ago.

"Getting yourself killed won't bring him back!" her mother had screamed. It was the worst fight they'd gotten into, and they'd not spoken for weeks afterward.

These days they were on much better terms, with their relationship improving once Adrian left law enforcement and went into academia. But there was still a gulf between them, a shared space of grief that neither of them had been able to breach.

She tucked away her phone, setting aside thoughts of her mother for the time being. Sebastian was missing, and the longer he wasn't found . . .

Adrian closed her eyes, trying to figure out what Sebastian had learned that would make someone want to abduct him. She knew that Sebastian was fascinated by the events that had occurred at the end of Cleopatra's life, especially the mystery of where she was buried. Cleopatra's tomb had never been found, with many historians concluding that the same cataclysmic tsunami that buried her famous palace beneath the waves of the Mediterranean may have also swept it out to sea.

Was that what Sebastian had discovered? The location of Cleopatra's tomb?

Her phone shrilled, jerking her from her thoughts. She looked down at it, surprised to see that it was Mira. She'd assumed it would take some time for her to call back.

"Adrian," Mira said, her voice sounding strained and out of breath.

Adrian sat up, even more alert now. "What's happened?"

"I sent my sister a text to check our apartment back in New York. She just got back to me. It-it's been ransacked. She called the police and they're over there now."

Adrian closed her eyes, her heart pounding. Whoever did this had international connections. How far did all of this go?

"Was anything taken?"

"They're still cataloging things, so I don't know yet," Mira said. "Oh my God, Adrian. What the hell was Sebastian involved in?"

"That's what I'm trying to find out."

"I was looking through all my recent texts from Sebastian, and he mentioned he keeps copies of his notes in a hiding place for every temporary office he works out of. He's always paranoid about losing his handwritten notes. Have you searched his office in Rome?"

Adrian stilled. She knew of Sebastian's wariness about losing the notes that he insisted on writing by hand; she didn't know he kept copies in his temporary offices. She and Nick had checked his office but not any potential hiding spots. What if they had missed something?

"I'll check again."

"Just find him, Adrian," Mira said, her voice wavering. "Please."

Adrian hung up, her pulse racing. If Sebastian had notes hidden in his office . . .

Adrian called Nick, but it went right to voicemail. She tried again, only for the call to go to voicemail once more.

She gritted her teeth with frustration; if her memory served her correctly, meetings with superiors could drag on for hours during high-profile investigations.

Time was something she didn't have the benefit of.

Sending Nick a quick text, Adrian headed out of the office.

~

Rome, Italy
4:58 A.M.

ADRIAN WAS SURPRISED to find the electronically secured front doors to the university unlocked when she arrived at the American University of Rome, and no sign of the security guard.

Alarm skittered through her, and she wished she had a weapon. But worry for Sebastian propelled her forward; she kept careful track of her surroundings as she hurried down the long corridor and up the stairs, making her way to Sebastian's office.

The door was closed, just as she and Nick had left it, but she still pressed her ear to the door, listening for any sound. Hearing only silence, she pushed open the door and stepped inside.

Moving to the desk, she knelt down, scanning underneath it for anything out of the ordinary. There was nothing on the floor. When she looked up, she froze, spotting a file folder taped to the underside of the desk.

Relief filled her, and as she reached for it—

She stilled at the sound of footsteps approaching from the outside corridor. Clutching the file folder, Adrian leapt to her feet, reaching for a paperweight perched on the edge of Sebastian's desk as a makeshift weapon, and scurried into the storage closet next to the desk.

She waited, her heart in her throat, as the door swung open. She heard footsteps entering, and the sound of paper rustling as the intruder looked through Sebastian's paperwork. Adrian looked down at the paperweight in her hand, wondering if she could use the element of surprise to her advantage . . . when the footsteps made their way to the storage closet.

Adrian held her breath, clutching the paperweight, waiting. The silence seemed to stretch until—

Her cell shrilled, shattering the silence.

The door swung open. A large, brutish-looking man stood there, glaring at her.

They moved at the same time. The man lunged

for her, and Adrian dodged, swinging the paper-weight at his head. The man tumbled to the ground, howling in pain, before reaching out with his foot to knock her to the floor.

Adrian landed on her back, the wind momentarily knocked from her lungs. The man straddled her, his hands reaching for her throat, and Adrian lifted her knee, sending her kneecap into his crotch.

He hissed in pain, and his fist slammed into Adrian's face, his other hand going to her throat. As he began to squeeze, Adrian heard a commotion coming from down the hall—frantic shouts in Italian.

And they were close.

The man cursed, slamming Adrian's head down hard once more before he shot to his feet, darting to the window and climbing out.

Clutching her head and reeling in pain, Adrian stumbled to her feet and charged after him. She was climbing out the window when the door to Sebastian's office burst open behind her, and frantic shouts rang out in both English and Italian—*Stop! Fermare!*—but her entire focus was on the intruder, who was now racing across the courtyard.

Ignoring the shouts, she climbed out of the window, using the metal trellis to climb down. She darted across the courtyard, but the intruder was no longer in sight, having disappeared beyond the gates that surrounded the courtyard.

Still, she ran, determined to catch up with him,

but a body slammed into her from behind, holding her still.

"Damn it, Adrian!" Nick shouted. "The university security guard was found dead, and the police think you're an intruder—running away isn't helping. Hold still. You're only going to make things worse."

"The actual intruder is getting away!" Adrian shouted, frustration surging through her.

Nick turned to the uniformed officers behind him, shouting in Italian and gesturing at the gates that surrounded the courtyard. They immediately darted forward, this time with Nick and Adrian on their heels, but by the time they all tore out of the courtyard through the rear gates onto the street, there was no sign of the intruder.

He was gone.

And so was the only link to Sebastian.

CHAPTER 9

Rome, Italy
5:26 A.M.

*A*drian leaned against the wall of the courtyard, watching as Nick spoke to the local Italian authorities, adrenaline still buzzing through her veins.

The intruder had murdered the young security guard who worked nights at the university, explaining why the door was left unlocked. They'd found his body in a nearby janitor's closet; the intruder had shot him in the chest. During the struggle, the guard had triggered the silent alarm which sent the police to the university. Nick had gotten her text and arrived at the same time as the local police.

The authorities were searching the grounds and the surroundings for the intruder based on the description she'd given, but so far, they hadn't found a trace of him.

Adrian knew he was long gone.

Another wave of frustration swept over her. Was the intruder the man who'd abducted Sebastian, or was he just one of many? She closed her eyes, clenching her fists at her sides to quell her anger. Sebastian's notes that she'd found hadn't been very helpful; they were just notes sketching out a timeline about Cleopatra's last days, and she already knew that Sebastian was fascinated by the Egyptian queen's last days.

Nick approached her, his expression grim, and she thought she saw him subtly shake his head. His boss, Jeremy Briggs, trailed him. Briggs was a sour-faced man who had FBI written all over him, from the rigid way he carried himself to the natural gleam of suspicion in his dark eyes.

Nick's mouth was set in a firm line as he approached; he'd been short with her ever since he'd arrived on the scene. She knew he was upset she'd come here alone and endangered the investigation.

"Miss West," Briggs said coolly. "I've been looking over the report you gave to the police. You said you didn't see the guard when you arrived."

"Yes," she said, trying to hide her impatience. Why was he repeating information he already knew? They needed to be focused on locating the intruder, the one link they had to Sebastian. She looked at Nick, but he was stone-faced.

"And you didn't see any sign of a struggle?" Briggs pressed.

"No," Adrian said shortly.

"You didn't find that odd?"

"I did, but I was too focused on finding anything that could help locate Sebastian."

Briggs stared at her for a long moment before continuing. "Why did you come here alone?"

"Sebastian's wife told me he may have notes hidden in his office—something that could explain why he was abducted. I didn't want to risk the time waiting for Agent Harper to finish his meeting."

"And you didn't notice anything when you came to search the office earlier with Agent Harper?"

There was no mistaking the suspicious edge to his voice. She looked at Nick, but he still wasn't looking at her, his gaze fixed on some point on the horizon.

"No," she said, trying to maintain her calm. "I obviously missed something."

"Agent Harper tells me you spoke to Roberta Fields earlier this evening," Briggs continued. "Do you know her personally?"

Adrian stiffened. Why was he asking her about Roberta?

"Yes, she used to be a professor of mine."

"And you went to talk to her because . . . "

Again, she looked at Nick. Hadn't he told him all of this? Briggs' voice had a sharp edge as he said, "I'm asking the questions, not Agent Harper."

"She was planning to meet with Sebastian. We wanted to see if she knew anything that might explain why someone would want to take him," Adrian said, struggling to maintain her patience.

"Why are you helping with the search?"

"Sebastian is a close friend of mine," she said tersely. "I promised his wife I'd help."

"You aren't an authorized investigator on this case. Agent Harper has been reprimanded for allowing you to accompany him."

She slid another glance at Nick, and this time she knew she didn't imagine it: he gave her a subtle shake of his head.

Tension gripped her. There was something else going on here.

"I apologize. Agent Harper isn't to blame. I insisted on helping with the investigation."

Briggs said nothing for several long moments, his gaze boring into her. It was another interrogation technique Adrian was very familiar with, making extensive eye contact with a perp until they were uncomfortable. But Adrian evenly held Brigg's gaze, unfazed.

"Were you aware," Briggs said finally, "that Roberta Fields was just found murdered in her home?"

CHAPTER 10

American University of Rome
5:31 A.M.

*A*drian stared at Briggs, stunned, as ice icy terror flooded her body. She recalled Roberta's caginess and her suspicion that she was hiding something.

"I'd like to ask you some more questions," Briggs said, his gaze still pinned to her face, "about your relationship with Sebastian Rossi."

Adrian stared at him in disbelief as a horrifying realization struck her, hitting her with the force of a bullet.

She knew exactly where this was leading. Briggs would imply that she was having an affair with Sebastian. Jealous of his relationship with Roberta, she had done away with the other woman.

It was an utterly ridiculous theory, and a reminder of one of the things she'd disliked about law enforcement. The need to tie everything up into a neat bow, to force square theories into round holes.

But . . . she *was* the last person to have seen Roberta alive. There must be city surveillance cameras on the street near where Roberta lived, showing that Nick had left her and Roberta alone. Whoever had actually murdered Roberta must have used a rear entrance not covered by the cameras.

Adrian hesitated. She could refuse, but that would only make her look guilty. Yet if the authorities focused on her instead of Sebastian's actual abductor, it would only stall the search.

Before she could answer, Nick spoke for her. "I'll take her back to headquarters," he said, still not looking at Adrian.

Disbelief and an odd sense of betrayal struck her at Nick's words, but he still avoided her eyes. Briggs didn't respond, keeping his intent gaze trained on Adrian's face.

Adrian schooled her features to a neutral expression, used to this game. "I'll be happy to talk," she said, keeping her tone even.

"Good," Briggs replied, giving her a tight, wintry smile and a brief nod to Nick before turning to walk away.

She waited until Briggs was out of earshot before turning to face Nick.

"Nick—" she began.

"Not here," he said sharply. "We don't have much time. Come with me."

As Nick walked back with Adrian to his car, he kept outwardly calm, but internally he was reeling.

He'd learned of Roberta's murder during his briefing with Briggs. He'd wanted to get to the scene immediately, but Briggs had stopped him, asking him probing questions about Adrian. That's when he'd learned that Briggs considered Adrian a suspect.

He'd tried to convince Briggs that his notion was ridiculous. Adrian was no murderer, but Briggs had seemed determined to follow through on his theory. He was even suspicious of her having a possible role in the security guard's murder, noting it was interesting that he was found dead around the time of Adrian's arrival. The security camera footage from the lobby where the guard's murder had occurred had been tampered with, so they only had Adrian's word to go on.

Given the timing of Roberta's murder, he suspected that whoever had kidnapped Sebastian was also behind both murders, proving that Roberta was indeed hiding something—likely her link to Sebastian's abductor. If Briggs and the local authorities were focused on Adrian, the trail on Sebastian's abductor and Roberta's murderer would go cold . . . which would play right into the true murderer's hands.

Something that he and Adrian had always argued about when they were partners was her willingness—sometimes even eagerness—to bend the rules, while Nick usually followed the rules to a tee.

Well, this was a pretty good time to bend the rules.

He'd come up with a solution as he and Briggs had driven to the American University of Rome. He'd been short with Adrian so she'd think he was upset about her coming here alone . . . and he was. She could have gotten herself killed, the stubborn woman, but he also needed to buy them time.

Once they got to her car, Adrian turned to him, her hazel eyes filled with anger. But Nick held up his hand.

"I know what you're thinking, and I agree. Briggs is full of it. I'm not taking you back to the embassy. We're going to find out who's really behind all this."

ADRIAN STARED at her former partner, relief flooding her. He'd always had her back. She should have known his coldness was an act for Briggs. Still, she wouldn't let him put his job and reputation on the line for her.

"I can't let you do that," she insisted. "Go back

to the office, say I got the slip on you. I'm going to handle this on my own."

"Nope," Nick said simply, starting the car and pulling away.

"Nick—"

"I know how stubborn you are, Adrian, but I can be just as stubborn. I've already made up my mind. This is my decision. When it's time, I'll deal with Briggs."

Adrian fell silent. She knew it was no use arguing with Nick. He was right, he could be just as stubborn as she was—even more so. And despite her misgivings, she couldn't help but feel another surge of relief. It felt good to have Nick as an ally and partner again.

"Where are we going?"

"Well, we don't have much time," Nick said. "Briggs is going to quickly realize I didn't take you back to the embassy, so your hotel or my apartment here aren't options. We're going to need to ditch this car and find somewhere safe until we figure out what's next."

"Did Vince find anything on Roberta Fields?" she asked, her mind racing.

"I didn't have time to check with him. I was with Briggs debriefing him when we learned of Roberta's murder. He's probably still looking into it. He would have told me if he'd found anything," Nick said, frustration flickering across his face.

"The Italian authorities are checking surveillance cameras around the university. Hopefully, they also haven't been tampered with," Nick added. "I can ask Vince to pass along any info—his girlfriend is an Italian cop."

"Even though you're on the run with a murder suspect?"

"I don't know if you noticed, but Vince isn't necessarily by the book," Nick said, offering her a rueful grin. "And he's not the hugest fan of Briggs. He'll continue to help us out, even if it's under the radar."

Nick stopped at a red light, reaching into the glove compartment to take out a small black case and extracting a phone. At Adrian's inquiring look, he said, "A backup phone not linked to the bureau. It's untraceable. I've had it for years as a just-in-case."

"A just-in-case for when you need to go on the run with your former partner?" Adrian asked with a chuckle of disbelief. "What happened to my partner who was all about the rules?"

"Following the rules doesn't mean they can't be bent," Nick said, giving her a wink as he called to Vince, putting it on speaker.

"Vince," Nick said. "I can't talk for long. You'll soon find out why, but I trust you and I know you trust me."

"You're kind of scaring me, dude," Vince said.

"Sorry, man. Look, I know you're still digging into Roberta Fields' background, but I need another quick favor—off the record."

Nick asked him to pass along any information

into the search for the intruder, and to see if he could find out anything more about the burglary at Sebastian's apartment back in New York.

"Will do," Vince said. "And whatever's going on—stay safe."

Nick ended the call. Adrian prayed Vince could dig up something useful about Roberta's background or relay information from the surveillance cameras from this girlfriend of his. They needed something to go on, because right now, she still had more questions than answers.

Nick drove a few more blocks before parking the car on the side of the street. They were across from a subway station.

"I think we should hop a train to the Spanish Steps. We can blend in with the mob of tourists there."

Adrian nodded her agreement, thinking about the steps, located in the bustling center of the city. They comprised over one hundred steps leading from the Piazza di Spagna to the Piazza Trinità dei Monti, with the Trinità dei Monti church over-looking it all. With Rome itself receiving millions of tourists each year, the crowded Spanish Steps was the perfect tourist spot where they could blend in.

They exited the car and hurried across the street to the subway. Rome was just waking up, with commuters heading to and from the subway, shops opening, and street vendors setting up their wares.

If she were back in New York, Adrian would

just be waking, nursing her customary morning black coffee as she made last-minute tweaks to a lecture she was giving, answering emails from her students, or prepping for a trip to the research library. Her life since leaving law enforcement had been quiet, simple. A little boring, yes, but easy. It was what she'd wanted after her turbulent years with the bureau, without the enduring darkness of profiling murderers and serial killers hovering over her like a black cloud.

But now, she was a murder suspect on the run, searching for her abducted friend and colleague. Her gut clenched when she thought of this news reaching Mira, but Mira knew her—and her husband. She would never believe the FBI's attempt to concoct some affair between her and Sebastian, nor would she believe Adrian capable of murdering Roberta.

For a split second, Adrian wondered if she should go back to the embassy and clear her name, but time was of prime importance. The best way to prove her innocence was to find Sebastian and whoever had killed Roberta. She strongly suspected they were the same person or group of people. She couldn't do that if she was being detained on trumped-up charges by her former employer.

Adrian made a mental note to send Mira a secure message as soon as she could. Her thoughts strayed to the call she owed her mother, and she had to suppress the urge to laugh. If she'd thought her mother would be worried before, she'd *really* be worried now.

Hey Mom, I was nearly murdered by this intruder who broke into Sebastian's office—the same man who likely murdered two other people tonight. Oh, and I'm a suspect in said murders. How's your day going?

Besides, if she contacted her mother, she'd risk dragging her mother into her plight, and she refused to involve her.

As she and Nick rode the subway, Adrian's thoughts turned to Sebastian's notes. She'd been hasty when looking over them the first time, still running on adrenaline from her encounter with the intruder. Maybe she had overlooked something. Something vital.

When they emerged from the subway at the Spagna stop, she led Nick to an alley near the Spanish Steps. Though it was early, tourists were already making their way to the steps. Adrian reached for the file folder in her bag.

"I want to see if I missed something in Sebastian's notes," she explained, taking out the notes and carefully scanning each page.

Nothing jumped out at her, and she was just about to put the notes away when she noticed something.

It was written at the very bottom in Sebastian's messy scrawl . . . very easy to miss. A series of letters and numbers that looked like gibberish, but Adrian knew exactly what it was.

She looked up at Nick, a smile tugging at her lips. *Thank you, Sebastian.*

"What?" Nick asked, looking puzzled by her smile.

"I did miss something. At the bottom of Sebastian's notes . . . he wrote a code."

CHAPTER 11

Embassy of the United States - FBI Offices
Rome, Italy
6:27 A.M.

*B*riggs glared at his assistant in disbelief. "What do you mean, they're not here?"

His assistant, a flustered, pale-faced young man in his twenties, swallowed hard. "Agent Harper never arrived."

Anger and disbelief swelled in Briggs, and he struggled to calm himself. *They just haven't arrived yet.*

But even as he tried to reassure himself, he knew that wasn't true. It didn't take long to get to the embassy from the American University, especially given how light traffic was at this time of day. Which meant one thing.

Agent Harper had fled with Adrian West.

He gritted his teeth, leaving his flustered assistant behind to stalk to his office. He knew of Adrian West's reputation; she'd been one of the youngest and most successful criminal profilers during her time at Quantico. He'd heard the word "brilliant" many times when people referred to her, even though she was notorious for frequently getting in trouble with her superior for skirting the rules of protocol.

He'd briefly looked her up online and found that she was now a consulting professor and lecturer at New York University in ancient languages and manuscripts; she'd done several joint lectures with Sebastian Rossi over the years, lending even more credence to their closeness. On the surface, she did seem brilliant and accomplished for someone so young, but that didn't mean there wasn't darkness there.

There was her father's disappearance, not long before she joined the bureau, and that infamous last case that had seemed to prompt her resignation.

Briggs had long been suspicious of criminal profilers such as West. He preferred good old-fashioned detective work rather than psychological mumbo jumbo to find perps. In his opinion, in order to become a profiler, one had to be unnervingly good at understanding criminals.

Perhaps too good.

Briggs himself had been a pretty damn good detective before he'd joined the bureau. It was one reason he'd risen through the ranks and earned his position as head of Art Crimes.

He'd come to Rome to assist with the investigation into the stolen Cleopatra artifacts and had taken his best agents with him, including Nick Harper. While the murder of Roberta Fields was technically under Italy's jurisdiction, it was still the murder of an American citizen, and the main suspect at this point was a former FBI agent. Given that there was no real movement on the artifact case—there were many international agencies involved, with the turf wars to boot—his team had the time to spare.

The evidence against West, both circumstantial and otherwise, was growing. There was the death of the security guard, though that was harder to pin in terms of motive, unless the guard had refused to give her access to Sebastian's office. If that were the case, getting into Sebastian's office was of utmost importance to her. Perhaps there was some evidence there she wanted to get rid of, something that would link her to Roberta's murder—or Sebastian's disappearance?

Still, linking her to the guard's murder seemed more of a stretch. There was more linking her to Roberta's murder in terms of motive and opportunity. She was the last person seen on security cameras visiting Roberta Fields, and it didn't take much of a leap to make the connection for a motive. Jealousy.

Nick had told him that Adrian's relationship

with Sebastian was more akin to a father-daughter one than a friendship. But Briggs had his doubts about that. Student-professor affairs were all too common. West could have been jealous of Sebastian and Roberta's relationship. He'd heard rumors that West had a temper, almost coming to blows with several suspects when she was still with the FBI.

And now she had fled, along with one of his best agents. He knew Nick had been West's former partner, but he was firmly by the book. He never would have thought that Nick would do something like this. Hell, he considered him a friend.

He set his mouth in a grim line as he entered his office, sitting down to pick up the phone. Now was not the time for sentiment; it was time to bring in a suspect, along with the rogue agent who was assisting her in evading questioning.

"I need a search done," he told one of his agents, Michael Andrews, as soon as he answered. "We're looking for Agent Nick Harper and a suspect he has with him, Adrian West."

Spanish Steps
Rome, Italy
6:32 A.M.

ADRIAN STUDIED the letters at the bottom of Sebastian's notes, still smiling, her heart pumping with newfound adrenaline.

"It's a Caesar cipher," she said.

Named after Julius Caesar, who used it to conceal his messages, a Caesar cipher was a relatively simple substitution cipher.

"The cipher alphabet that Sebastian uses—the one he taught me, uses a left shift of four. So, the letter A is D, the letter B is E, and so on," she explained.

She studied the letters at the bottom of Sebastian's notes, which read:

UREHUWDF and **MXOLHQX**

She did a quick mental decoding. The letters translated to names.

ROBERTA F
JULIEN C

"Names," Nick said, when she told him the decoded message. "We know he was in contact with Roberta Fields. But who is Julien C?"

Adrian knew exactly who Julien C was. "Julien Caron," she replied.

Adrian had heard the name Julien Caron before. Sebastian had mentioned him several times; he had a bit of a reputation in the archaeological community.

Julien Caron was the son of an Egyptian archaeologist mother and wealthy French father who was a banker. Even though he'd inherited great wealth from his father's side, he'd chosen to go into archaeology, like his mother before him. He was young, handsome, charismatic, and appealed to millennials interested in ancient history, with an active social media presence and loads of followers, eschewing the stereotype of archaeologists as old and stuffy.

But most importantly, his specialty was Ptolemaic Egypt, with many of his digs being centered on finds from Cleopatra's illustrious family dynasty.

After briefly explaining to Nick who Julien was, she added, "If he was in contact with Julien, maybe Sebastian discovered—or had a lead on—Cleopatra's tomb. Maybe that's why he was taken. His abductors want him to lead them there. As for talking to Julien, we're in luck. He's attending the same conference as Sebastian and me. He's scheduled to speak at the conference in two days."

Using Nick's backup phone, Adrian did an internet search for Julien Caron's social media profiles, and found one of his most recent posts, showing the fancy hotel he was staying at in Rome.

"Over sharing millennials," Nick said, shaking his head.

"If it's so easy for us to find him, whoever abducted Sebastian can find him easily as well," Adrian said, unease growing in her gut.

"Then we have to get to him first," Nick returned, grim. "Let's go."

CHAPTER 12

Spagna Metro Station
Rome, Italy
6:40 A.M.

*L*eonid trailed Agent Nick Harper and Adrian West from a distance, watching as they emerged from the alleyway they'd tucked themselves away in and headed back to the subway. Yara's contact at the FBI had identified them for him, and his suspicions about them being law enforcement were mostly correct. Harper was a current FBI agent, while West was a former fed.

After his encounter with West, during which he should have just killed the bitch before the police's arrival had forced him to flee, he'd hidden himself by breaking into a home at the base of Janiculum Hill to avoid the police who were searching the area for him.

He'd called Yara to inform her he'd not found

anything else of note in Sebastian's office. When he'd reluctantly told her about his encounter with West, Yara had expressed relief that he hadn't killed her.

"The authorities are focused on her, and we need them to remain that way. If she's dead, that doesn't help us," Yara informed him. She'd ordered Leonid to keep his eye on them in case they got too close to discovering Sebastian's actual whereabouts. "I would trust no one but you with this," Yara added, her voice lowering to a seductive purr.

"Not even my brother?" Leonid asked, the jealous retort coming from his lips before he could stop it.

It doesn't matter now, he reminded himself. But resentment still simmered in his belly over how she seemed to rely on Markos more than him.

If his retort bothered Yara, she didn't show it. "No one but you, my *volk.*"

Volk. It was the Russian word for wolf, a word Yara had given him as a term of affection. She had used it the first time they'd made love.

But he knew Yara was using his lust to her advantage; he was no fool. *She's playing a role, as are you.*

It also reminded him of what was truly at stake, and the prize that awaited him.

His determination renewed, he slipped his cell phone into his pocket and slid his sunglasses on, turning to trail West and Agent Harper into the subway.

~

Hotel Agonisto
Rome, Italy
7:03 A.M.

JULIEN CARON WAS WORRIED.

He hadn't heard from Sebastian since last night, his messages and emails had gone unanswered. He also hadn't heard from Roberta Fields.

A dark premonition filled him as he made his way through the lobby of his luxury hotel, the lobby which he'd just filmed for his social media followers. He'd displayed his usual zany enthusiasm to his followers, but once he'd stopped filming, his worry had taken hold, a tingling sense of unease in his gut.

He recalled Sebastian's words to him only days before; his excitement tinged with nervousness. *It's just a theory,* Sebastian had told him. *Keep it quiet.*

And what a theory it was.

He took out his phone as he turned down the corridor that led to his room, sending Sebastian another text.

You're being paranoid, he told himself. *It's not been that long since he texted you.* Perhaps Sebastian was just busy preparing for another lecture he was giving at the conference or buried in his research.

Julien was so absorbed in his thoughts that he didn't notice someone following him. It was only when he used his key card to open his door that he looked up, a strangled cry erupting from his throat.

ADRIAN CAUTIOUSLY APPROACHED Julien Caron as he stumbled back, his eyes wide with fright as she and Nick entered his room behind him, holding their hands up to show they meant him no harm.

She'd been reluctant to approach him this way, but they didn't want to risk asking for him at the front desk.

"Who the hell are you?" Julien demanded, his shaky hand reaching down for his phone.

"Wait. Please—I'm sorry we had to approach you this way, but I swear to you we mean you no harm. I'm Adrian West, a friend of Sebastian Rossi's. This is Agent Nick Harper."

Julien stiffened in surprise, his hand still on his phone.

"Sebastian is missing," she continued, deciding to cut right to the chase. "He was abducted from his hotel room late last night. His colleague, Roberta Fields, was found murdered just hours ago."

The news seemed to be like a physical blow, and Julien staggered, sinking down onto the large bed.

She gave him several moments for this news to sink in before continuing. "I went to Sebastian's office and found his notes; he had your and Roberta's name written in code. He clearly didn't want just anyone to know he was in contact with you."

Julien went pale, burying his face in his hands. She decided not to add that she was currently the prime suspect in Roberta's murder; the news she'd just given him was more than enough for now.

Studying him, Adrian realized he didn't look so much surprised as he did scared. "Julien," she said, leaning forward. "I think you know why he was abducted . . . and why Roberta was murdered."

Julien swallowed hard, but still said nothing.

"Please. Sebastian is in grave danger. And given what happened to Roberta, I suspect you're in danger too."

Julien finally looked up at her. He expelled a sharp breath, raking his hand through his dark hair.

"A few days ago, Sebastian reached out to me with a theory," he said. "He believes that everything we know about Cleopatra's last days is wrong. He believes she didn't die in her mausoleum as the Romans recorded it. He believes she survived."

CHAPTER 13

Hotel Agonisto
Rome, Italy
7:10 A.M.

*A*stonishment coursed through Adrian at Julien's words. She and Sebastian had discussed Cleopatra at length, and he'd never mentioned such a theory.

Besides, historians agreed that Cleopatra died shortly before Rome annexed Egypt, though the method of her death—a dramatic bite from a snake or poison—remained a point of contention among some.

She was very aware of the official story of the end of Cleopatra's life. After she and Marc Antony lost the Battle of Actum to the future Roman emperor Augustus, she had locked herself in her mausoleum in Alexandria with her most trusted servants and killed herself not long after the Roman army entered Egypt.

Sebastian had told her many times that he didn't trust the Roman accounts of the end of Cleopatra's life, but he'd never given her any alternative scenarios.

Why hadn't he told her this theory? Did he not trust her?

"Wait. So you're saying that Cleopatra didn't commit suicide? She lived until old age or—" Nick began.

"No, not at all," Julien said, holding up a hand and shaking his head. "She certainly died not too long after Rome's annexation of Egypt—history would have told us otherwise, as she would have certainly left her mark. Sebastian's theory is that she lived *longer* than what was officially recorded, perhaps a year, perhaps slightly longer. He believes she planned for a counterattack against Rome and fully intended to reclaim her country and kingdom.

"Did he have evidence for this theory?" Adrian asked.

"History itself was his evidence. Rome told its own story when it was the victor, as it often was. Think about it. Cleopatra had been a formidable enemy, a strong ruler who'd held sway with two powerful Roman military leaders—Julius Caesar and then Marc Antony. On top of that, she was a woman. Once Cleopatra was out of the picture, Rome made certain to do a hit job on her and her legacy to discredit her. Something that frustrated

Sebastian, as I'm sure you're aware, Adrian, is how Cleopatra's intelligence is still to this day underestimated for this notion of her being this famed seductress."

Adrian nodded slowly, recalling how Sebastian expressed irritation with how Cleopatra was constantly portrayed. A wily, exotic seductress who used her sexuality to advance her power as opposed to the very intelligent and keen ruler that she was.

"Had she lived in modern times, she would have been considered a great head of state, controlling the massive and intricate Egyptian economy and the Ptolemaic wealth she'd inherited, which would equate to hundreds of millions of dollars today," Sebastian had told the audience at one of his guest lectures. "The Ptolemaic dynasty was full of treachery and danger, with the family killing its own members or Alexandrians deposing them. Cleopatra's own father was nearly deposed and only survived with the help of the Romans, something Cleopatra attempted to do herself, though it ultimately backfired. Furthermore," Sebastian had continued, "what's often left out of the stories of her 'seductions' is that both Caesar and Antony had multiple mistresses and affairs outside their marriages. Caesar was in his fifties when he met Cleopatra, while she was a young woman of twenty-one, yet she is the one painted as the seductress."

"So," Julien said now, pulling her back to the present, "what better way to end the story of this seductress queen by claiming she'd committed suicide by snake, a final act of cowardice with a flair of exoticism. They started that particular myth early. They paraded an effigy of her with an asp through the streets of Rome after her death."

"The snake thing didn't happen?" Nick asked, his eyebrows raised with curiosity.

Adrian hid a smile and leaned back. She'd lost count of how many times Sebastian had bemoaned the notion of Cleopatra committing suicide by the bite of an asp. She suspected Julien felt the same way, and by the irritated look that flitted across his features, she could tell that he did.

"For one thing, a snake would have been quite difficult to smuggle in amidst a basket of figs, as the tale often goes, and she was well-guarded during her final days. The bite of a snake was also less reliable than that of a far more painless means of death —poison," Julien said with a fierce scowl. "A simple deadly concoction of hemlock and opium would have done the deed, and Cleopatra's own uncle had committed suicide by poison; it was a method of suicide well-known to the Ptolemies, who were always on the cusp of mortal danger from their own subjects, the tumultuous Alexandrian court, or foreign invaders. But alas, the dramatic bite by an asp was a far more poetic end, and so the myth persists to this day."

Nick held up his hands in a gesture of apology and surrender, looking taken aback by Julien's passion. Julien's scowl faded, and he gave him a wary smile.

"Sorry, historians get caught up on some details like this. As I was saying, Sebastian has always been wary of the Roman account of the end of her life," Julien continued. "In fact, the two most used sources who wrote about the circumstances of her death—Plutarch and Dio—wrote about her one and two centuries after her death, respectively. These are the sources that tell us what most historians accept. After losing the Battle of Actum to Octavian, who goes on to become the Emperor Augustus, Antony commits suicide; Cleopatra commits suicide by a very dramatic snake bite; Rome annexes Egypt. The End. *But,*" Julien said, leaning forward, "minus those sources, we don't really know what happened other than that she disappears from the historical record. Sebastian believes that whatever happened, it wasn't the official Roman version. It wasn't until the artifacts belonging to Cleopatra's daughter were discovered that he thought he could find evidence for it."

"What evidence could there be in old jewels?" Adrian asked.

"Patience," Julien said, giving Adrian a smile. "I'm getting there. Now, Cleopatra was a very shrewd woman, and she was certainly aware of Rome's growing threat to Egypt and her rule. Sebastian believed she was prepared for possible defeat long before the battle of Actum. The

Ptolemies had massive wealth. Naturally, Cleopatra needed to protect that wealth."

Julien paused for a moment before continuing. "Knowing that Rome was coming, that her very kingdom was at stake, the Cleopatra Sebastian believes existed would have been prepared. He believes what happened after her 'death' is where things get . . . interesting. Her death marks the end of the Hellenestic Age, ushering in the Roman era. She develops a legacy of course, and history certainly doesn't forget her. But what Sebastian focused on was those early chaotic days after her death. What happened to those loyal to her? To Cleopatra's and Antony's bodies? And most importantly, what happened to all of that glorious wealth? Yes," he said, as Adrian started to answer, "of course Rome took the vast majority of it. Of that there is no doubt. With the treasures the Romans took from Cleopatra's palace and Egypt, the Roman economy soared."

Julien held their gazes for a long moment, and Nick said warily, "I take it there's another 'but' coming."

"You would be right," Julien said, grinning. "*But* Sebastian believes Cleopatra hid a great deal of her treasure and intended to use it to fund her counterattack."

He paused, holding their gazes.

"A treasure that's still out there to this day."

CHAPTER 14

*A*s Julien's words sank in, Adrian sat there, reeling at this possibility.

A lost treasure belonging to Cleopatra, waiting to be discovered.

"Again, Cleopatra was quite a shrewd woman. She had to know what was coming. Sebastian told me he believed she may have been prepared, that she wasn't ready to give up. The suicide by asp is too convenient an end for someone so determined. The Ptolemies were nothing but resourceful. As I mentioned before, her father was nearly run off the throne but returned with an army to take back his throne by force. Sebastian—and I—believe this may have occurred to Cleopatra. She had done it before, successfully hiring a mercenary army to fight against her brother when she was just twenty-one. If she had access to funds and could flee, it would simply be a matter of going to her loyal supporters, using her funds to raise an army, and to march against Rome. Defeat against Rome would have been difficult, yes, but not impossible."

"But she still disappears from the historical record," Adrian said, shaking her head. "Like you said, if she survived longer, there would have been some mention of it."

"Agreed," Julien said. "While Sebastian believes she survived longer than is officially documented, he doesn't believe she lived long enough to make an impact. She still met her end —perhaps by suicide, perhaps by a Roman assassin who found her and dispatched her—but she was still prepared. Remember, when she died, she still had four surviving children, three of whom were sons. Two were sons of Marc Antony, another a son of Julius Caesar. Men with supporters who would have gladly marched to support their sons. We know Cleopatra promoted her son by Caesar, Caesarion, to take her place; she even held an elaborate coming-of-age party for him in Alexandria after the battle of Actum. Not the actions of a queen ready to admit defeat, but someone making a statement that the Ptolemies would continue to rule Egypt, even without her."

Adrian considered this. Cleopatra couldn't have known that Caesarion, her oldest, was killed when his tutor betrayed her for Roman favor, nor that her son, Ptolemy Philadelphus, would die young, and her other son, Alexander Helios, would later disappear. Many historians assumed Augustus murdered him, not wanting to risk the possibility of the son of Marc Antony rising against him.

"Yet when it comes to Cleopatra's children, many people forget about Cleopatra's daughter, Cleopatra Selene, as is sadly too common with women of antiquity. Her daughter was the only one of her children to survive into adulthood. She married a king and had a family of her own, continuing the line of Cleopatra."

"Sebastian thinks her daughter had access to this treasure? If so, why didn't she use it as her mother intended?" Nick asked.

"Sebastian thinks Selene never accessed it. He has theories as to why. One is that she knew it was futile to fight against Rome. Another is that she became close to the woman who raised her, the Emperor Augustus' sister, and perhaps even to Augustus himself, and didn't want to risk the danger of seeking such a treasure and suffering their wrath. Augustus certainly didn't seem to view Selene as a threat; he married her off to a client king he seemed to have a close relationship with. But there is another theory . . . a far more intriguing one," he continued. "And that is that the treasure was never found. If this theory is true, that means the treasure is still out there. So, when the artifacts were found, belonging to Cleopatra's daughter . . ."

"Sebastian believes there's some clue within them, something leading to this treasure. Something that Cleopatra would have left for her daughter, *knowing* that the patriarchal Roman society wouldn't consider her a threat," Adrian finished for him.

If this were true, Cleopatra had been prescient, given that her daughter was the only one of her children to survive into adulthood.

"This would all explain why Sebastian was taken," she continued, her pulse thrumming. "Whoever abducted him thinks he has some knowledge of where this treasure can be."

Julien gave her a grim nod. Adrian leaned back in her chair, exhaling a sigh. They now had a tantalizing possibility for the reason of Sebastian's abduction but still no clue as to his whereabouts.

She reached up to wearily rub her temples— when she spotted a movement out of the corner of her eye.

Adrian stilled, turning to face the courtyard. There, she glimpsed a figure. It was just a glimpse, but she recognized him.

It was the same man she'd fought with at Sebastian's office.

"Nick," she hissed, already on her feet. "The intruder at Sebastian's office—he's out there."

She didn't wait for him to reply, pushing open the patio door and darting out after the intruder, blood pumping furiously through her veins.

CHAPTER 15

Unknown
7:25 A.M.

*Y*ara watched Doctor Rossi on the security monitor before her, taking in his look of awe.

A part of Yara admired him for being able to push past his fear and allow awe to sweep over him, to take in items that the great Cleopatra herself had once worn. She'd felt the same way when she'd taken the artifacts in, along with a sense of responsibility. She knew the artifacts could change everything for her and the organization.

"Yara . . . "

Yara started. She'd almost forgotten that Fairuza stood behind her, hovering next to Markos, whose gaze was intently trained on the monitor.

Fairuza glanced at the monitor before returning her gaze to Yara's. "Was—was this necessary? To abduct the professor. Couldn't we have just asked for his help?"

Irritation and anger filled Yara, and she took several deep breaths to calm herself.

"You know we will do what we must to help our organization reach its goals. I couldn't risk exposing myself, nor our organization, to the professor. Do I need to remind you that Cleopatra herself was forced to murder her own siblings to stay alive?"

Fairuza paled. "Are—are you saying that you intend to—"

"You knew the rules when you joined us, what lengths we'll go to. Are you questioning my authority?"

"No—goddess, no," Fairuza said quickly, looking shame-faced. "I-I was just wondering if there was another way—"

"There isn't," Yara said bluntly. "Question me again, and I'll have you scrubbing toilets with the new initiates. Understood?"

Fairuza ducked her head, her eyes brimming with tears.

A sliver of regret crept through Yara, one that she pushed away. She'd been too tolerant of Fairuza's hesitancy with some of the organiza-tion's methods because the young woman reminded her of herself when she was younger. Now that they were so close to obtaining a trea-sure that could change everything, she couldn't risk such hesitancy from one of her top associates.

It was time to stop treating Fairuza with kid gloves.

You had your own doubts too, at first, a niggling voice whispered. *And Dalal was patient with you.*

She could still remember when she'd first learned about the secret society—the organization she now led—the Daughters of Cleopatra. Dalal, tending to the bruises on her face and battered body, had told her about it in hushed, reverent tones.

"The Daughters is a secret society that began in the early days after Cleopatra's fall to restore her heirs to power and overthrow the tyranny of Rome. In ancient times, it failed to restore her heirs to power, but it played a hand in several successful uprisings against Rome. By the time of Rome's fall, the group had dwindled and fractured, but a small splinter group remained in Egypt, rising unsuccessfully against the Arab conquest. Other splinter and fracture groups focused on overthrowing tyranny throughout the ages. But the original group has remained in Egypt, still devoted to Cleopatra's legacy," Dalal had said.

Yara had reeled at the knowledge of this. When her body had fully healed, she had delved into all the literature that Dalal gave her about Cleopatra and the goddess she had associated herself with, a deity the Daughters still worshipped, Isis.

As Dalal told her more about the group and their plans, Yara thought of all that she had been through.

She came from a wealthy family in Cairo, and she had married a handsome young man from another wealthy family. It wasn't long after their marriage that her new husband had began to beat her.

When she showed up to family dinners with a bruised face, her parents had told her to stop provoking him, and when she'd gone to the police in desperation, they'd simply gone through the motions of filing her complaint before sending her right back to her furious husband, who punished her brutally for reporting him.

It was after a beating that nearly left her blind in one eye and with several broken ribs that she'd lain in a hospital bed, praying for death. Dalal had appeared in her room like an avenging angel, telling her she could take her away from her husband so that he and her uncaring family could never find her. All she had to do was to say the word. Yara had whispered, desperately, "Yes. Please."

She thought of the legions of women who had suffered beneath the yoke of patriarchal societies all over the world, not just at the hands of abusive partners, but of abusive societal practices that continued to oppress them. So when Dalal had taken her under her wing and asked if she wanted to join them, she had pledged herself and her life to the society, to make life better for women everywhere, to give them their rightful place in the world —especially in the Middle East.

Any hesitancy she'd had was gone by the time

she'd performed her first execution, that of a member who had gone against the sacred tenets of the society and revealed its secrets to an outsider. Her commitment was even more solidified when she had the honor of looking into the eyes of her former husband, her own personal abuser and oppressor, as she sank a knife into his heart.

Now, she looked at Fairuza, whose head was still bowed low. She moved toward her, tipping her head back to make her look into Yara's eyes.

"I've been too patient with you," she said with a sigh. "When it's time to dispose of the professor, I'll have you do the honors. It will solidify your commitment to the Daughters, as such an act once solidified mine."

7:30 *A.M.*

SEBASTIAN GAZED down at the precious artifacts with both trepidation and awe.

His abductor had also provided him with a small digital microscope to inspect the items, but he hadn't touched it yet, taking it all in with his naked eye.

They were even more stunning in person; the lapis lazuli earrings, the pendants, and the amethyst ring . . . all belongings of the most famous woman in antiquity.

Ever since the announcement of their find, he'd

dreamed of this moment, of looking at them in person, though under very different circumstances.

His thoughts turned to his theory; the theory that had gotten him into this mess. The theory he'd shared with just two people, Roberta Fields and Julien Caron.

He believed Cleopatra left a treasure behind for her children, one that could fund an army to continue the fight against Rome and restore the Ptolemaic dynasty. If his theory was correct, there could be some clue as to where it was hidden in something she bequeathed to her children. When he'd learned of the discovery of the artifacts, he'd known it was a long shot, but he thought that perhaps there would be a clue among them. Some indication that there was a treasure out there, some clue Cleopatra had left to her children, away from the prying eyes of the Romans.

When the artifacts were stolen, he'd hoped it was just a thief looking to sell the precious valuables on the black market, but now he knew how wrong he'd been.

Yet as he studied the artifacts, he saw nothing that indicated a secret message. His long shot theory had proved to be worth nothing, and now he and his family would suffer for it.

He closed his eyes, despair gripping him, despair which he forced aside. If there was nothing here, perhaps he could make something up. Give his abductors something, buy himself more time to figure out how to escape, or for the authorities to find him.

As he mulled over what he would say, his gaze landed on Cleopatra's famed amethyst ring. His eyes dropped to the stone, and to the one place he hadn't looked.

Anticipation filled him. He hated to deface such a precious artifact, but he had no choice. His family's lives depended on it.

Taking a deep breath, he looked up at the camera and waved his hand. After several moments, his abductor entered, scowling.

"I need to check beneath the stone. I need a pick of some kind," he said. His abductor gave him a long, suspicious look. "I'm telling the truth," Sebastian continued, holding up the ring. "I need to check beneath the stone. It's the one place I haven't looked."

The man left with a grunt, and when he returned, he had a miniature pick and a gun. Fear swelled over Sebastian as his abductor aimed the gun at his head as he handed Sebastian the pick. He said nothing, but the threat was there.

One wrong move and he was dead.

Sebastian took the pick, his hand shaking. He had to calm himself as he used the pick to carefully dislodge the stone from the ring.

He froze, his heart leaping into his throat as he looked down at the space beneath the stone.

There was a message inscribed there.

~

Embassy of the United States - FBI Offices
Rome, Italy
7:40 A.M.

"You're telling me that your top agent and a former agent—who is the prime suspect for a murder—have somehow slipped from your grasp?" shouted Charles Wyatt, the assistant director of the International Operations Division of the FBI, and one of Briggs' bosses, from the other end of the line.

Briggs closed his eyes, stifling a sigh. He'd been reluctant to update his boss back in DC on the Roberta Fields investigation; they were already unhappy with him for the lack of movement with the stolen artifacts. But he'd figured it was best if they heard it directly from him.

His reluctance had turned out to be justified.

"Yes," he replied, trying to keep his tone calm, "but I have both the local authorities and the agents here at the embassy searching for them. It's only a matter of time before—"

"They both need to be found yesterday, Agent Briggs. And keep this quiet. We don't need the press getting wind of this; it's embarrassing enough that we've made no progress with the Cleopatra artifacts. I want you to keep me updated every goddamn second. Understood?"

"Understood, sir."

Wyatt ended the call, and Briggs leaned back in

his chair. He eyed the decanter of whiskey on a shelf in the corner of his office, tempted to take a drink, but he needed to be fully alert to bring in his rogue agent and West.

As he forced his gaze away from the tempting whiskey and stood, Agent Andrews entered, looking flushed and out of breath.

"What is it?" Briggs asked sharply.

"We have a lead on Agent Harper and Adrian West's location," he said. "Surveillance just picked them up going into Hotel Agonisto."

CHAPTER 16

Hotel Agonisto
Rome, Italy
7:42 A.M.

*A*drian and Nick darted across the courtyard. The intruder had already raced through a second set of doors on the opposite side of the courtyard. They picked up their speed, shoving open the doors and hurrying out.

These doors led to a small side street that turned into an alleyway. Adrian glimpsed the intruder as he raced down it.

"Go around the other side—we can cut him off!" Adrian shouted.

Nick obliged, turning to run in the opposite direction as Adrian ran into the alley after the intruder. Her heart pumped with both adrenaline and fear as she ran; she was in pretty good shape, having a daily five-mile run in the mornings before classes. Still, this speed was testing her stamina. Yet she knew that if she lost the intruder this time, she might not get another chance and forever lose the link to Sebastian.

With this in mind, she picked up her pace, forcing her legs to move as fast as they could.

As she neared the end of the alley, she could see that the intruder was already at the far end, getting close to the street, too far for her to reach in time. *He's going to disappear again.* She moved as fast as her legs would go, but they weren't fast enough.

He was getting away.

Nick darted into the alley from the opposite end, cutting him off. Relief tore through her as he ran toward the man, replaced by panic as the intruder reached into his back pocket. *Gun.*

"Nick!" she shouted, but he was prepared, kicking out at the man's knees and sending him to the ground, where he quickly disarmed him.

As Adrian reached them, Nick placed his knee on the man's chest, pressing his gun to the side of his temple

"It's over," Nick growled.

MOMENTS LATER, the intruder sat opposite them, tied up securely to one of the hotel room chairs, not even looking remotely perturbed by the gun Adrian had leveled at his chest.

The alleyway had thankfully been empty as they'd dragged him back to the hotel. A pale-faced Julien had been waiting for them by the rear entry, leading them back to his room.

When they'd returned to Julien's room, Adrian and Nick had secured him in the chair with Nick's handcuffs.

"Who is he?" Julien asked now, his voice shaking. "Aren't you going to call the police? Security?"

"Not yet," Adrian said curtly, keeping her gaze trained on the man, who glared defiantly back at her. "Who are you?"

The man said nothing, his expression both stone-faced and hostile. Adrian studied him, doing a quick profile. Given his steadfast calm and the meticulous manner in which he'd abducted Sebastian—and she was convinced that he'd either been the one to abduct Sebastian or was a part of the team that had—he was a mercenary, a professional through and through.

Questioning wouldn't work on him.

She made an executive decision. She moved close to the man, who didn't even flinch, lifted the gun, and slammed it down onto his temple as hard as she could.

The man slumped over, unconscious. Nick let out a curse, and Julien gasped.

"Is that a new form of questioning?" Nick demanded, his eyebrows raised.

"He was never going to talk to us. Attempting to question him would have only wasted time."

She leaned forward, rummaging through the man's pockets and taking out his phone. According to a text sent to him from a blocked number, the only text there was, his name was Leonid. The text itself was no help. It merely stated: *Keep me updated*. There were also no contacts listed in his phone.

But there was the record of a last number dialed. Hope flared in her chest at the sight. If they could trace the location of this number, it could lead to his employer . . . to Sebastian.

Seeming to read her mind, Nick took the phone. "Let me call Vince and see if he can trace the number," he said, turning to head toward the patio.

Behind her, Julien looked at the unconscious Leonid and swallowed. "Adrian . . . what's really going on here? I think I have the right to know."

Adrian faced him, taking in his tense expression. There was no point now in withholding the truth.

"You might want to sit down," she said, and proceeded to tell Julien everything that had happened since she'd received the phone call from Nick in her hotel room late last night. The more she spoke, the paler Julien became.

"I'm not going to drag you even further into this. I only came to you because of Sebastian's coded message. We'll leave, and you can contact the FBI at the US Embassy for protection. I don't know if he was following us or is after you, but you may be in danger. All I want is to find Sebastian alive."

Julien met her gaze, seeming to see the truth of her words in her eyes. His fear seemed to vanish, replaced with determination.

But before he could reply, Nick entered, his mouth set in a grim line.

"We have to go. Now," he said. "Vince just gave me the heads up. My employer knows we're here—and they're coming."

CHAPTER 17

"*I*'m coming with you," Julien said.

Both Adrian and Nick turned to face Julien. "Julien—" Adrian began, shaking her head.

"You said that I'm in danger too."

"Yes," Adrian replied, "but the FBI can—"

"I may have just met you, but I know Sebastian. He speaks of you like you're a daughter to him. I can tell how much you care about him. I care about him too. Sebastian's been abducted and Roberta murdered. I don't want to just be a sitting duck. I may not have the breadth of Sebastian's knowledge about Cleopatra, but I know a great deal about her and her final days. I can help you. I know it in my gut. Please."

Adrian could see both the desperation and determination in his eyes and knew that, like Nick, there would be no swaying him. She sighed, giving Nick a look of resignation. Despite not wanting to

117

bring Julien into any more danger, she knew he was right; it would only help to have a Cleopatra expert with them as they searched for Sebastian, who was linked to this mysterious treasure.

"Fine," Adrian said. "But Nick's right. We have to go—now."

"What do we do with him?" Nick asked, gesturing to Leonid.

"It's not ideal, but we should take him with us. Even if he refuses to talk, he's our only solid lead to Sebastian, and we can possibly use him for leverage with the people he's working for," Adrian said.

"There's another back entrance out of the hotel, a secret one used by the more VIP guests. The manager showed it to me when I checked in," Julien informed them. "Hotel security usually has a guard standing there. I can distract him while you get to my car."

Adrian looked at Julien, surprised at the lengths he was already willing to go to help them. Seeming to read her mind, Julien held her gaze. "I'm all in on this. For Sebastian, Roberta—and myself," he said firmly.

They moved quickly. Julien gave them his keys and let them know the make and model of his car, and where it was parked in the adjoining garage, before leaving ahead of them to distract the guard.

After he left, Adrian and Nick hefted up Leonid, with Nick shouldering most of his weight. As they struggled with his muscular girth, Nick shot Adrian an annoyed look. "You know, your whole knocking him unconscious thing might not have been the best idea."

"He would have been next to impossible to get out of here if he was conscious," Adrian shot back.

Peering out before they left, they headed out of Julien's room with Leonid between them, moving as quickly as they could with his bulk. To her dread, a young couple came out of their room, blinking in surprise at the sight of them. Nick's suit jacket covered Leonid's handcuffs, so Adrian gave them a smile that she hoped looked rueful.

"Some people just can't hold their alcohol," she quipped as she and Nick maneuvered the intruder past them.

Fortunately, they were the only passersby they spotted; Julien's room was mercifully close to the secret back entrance. When they arrived, the door was open, and neither the guard nor Julien were anywhere in sight. *Thank you, Julien.*

Moving as quickly as they could, they made their way to the adjoining parking garage, Adrian using the same quip about Leonid being unable to hold his alcohol to the few passersby they passed, but she didn't know how much longer the excuse would hold up.

They soon spotted Julien's car, a sleek black Audi. Adrian unlocked the door, opening it for Nick to heft Leonid into the back seat, setting him upright so he just looked like a sleeping man. He jabbed his gun into Leonid's side as Adrian slid into the driver's seat.

Come on, she silently pleaded as they waited for Julien. It would be only minutes before the feds and local authorities arrived at the hotel.

To her relief, Julien arrived at the car only a minute later, sliding into the passenger's seat.

Heart hammering, Adrian started the car and peeled out of the garage.

~

7:55 *A.M.*

BRIGGS HURRIED down the hotel corridor, trailed by Andrews, a local police officer, and hotel security.

They'd arrived only moments earlier, gaining access to the hotel security cameras, where they'd spotted West and Nick heading into a guest by the name of Julien Caron's room, only to find them all leaving again, this time with the unconscious form of a large man.

He'd already sent several officers out to the parking garage, where it looked like they were heading, and another to interview the security guard who'd last spoken to Julien Caron before they'd fled. He'd ordered every inch of the hotel and the surroundings searched, but he already knew in his gut that Nick and West were in the wind. They both knew better than anyone what investigative search protocols looked like.

Once they arrived at Caron's room, the burly

hotel security guard knocked several times to no answer. Only then did he use his key card to open the door.

Briggs entered the luxurious hotel room, taking it in. Why had they come here to see Caron?

"I want to find out everything we can on this Julien Caron. I want to know how he's connected to Adrian West," Briggs told Andrews.

He moved to the center of the room, frowning. If he were trying to evade the authorities after committing murder, he would attempt to leave the country, not come to a high-end hotel to bring along someone else for the ride.

Something else was going on here, something that went beyond Roberta Fields' murder and Sebastian Rossi's disappearance.

And he was determined to find out what it was.

CHAPTER 18

Rome, Italy
8:04 A.M.

"Where are we going?" Julien asked as they sped away from Hotel Agonisto, continually checking the rearview mirror.

"We need to get as far away from the hotel as possible. The authorities are going to set up a perimeter," Adrian replied.

She glanced in the rearview mirror at Leonid, still slumped over and unconscious. Anger flared in her gut; this man knew where Sebastian was . . . or he was the one who'd taken him.

But why would he be following them? Were they close to finding Sebastian, and he was he trying to stop them?

Now that they had him in their custody, what exactly were they going to do with him? Using him as leverage would only work if his employer knew they had him, but he could very well be expendable.

Nick's phone chimed, pulling her from her anxious thoughts, and he answered, putting the call on speaker so they all could hear. Vince's voice came on over the line.

"The last call your guy made pinged at a tower near a farmhouse just outside of Rome. I'll send you a text with the address. I also have updates for you about Roberta Fields," Vince continued. "I found some interesting tidbits. She had a messy divorce a couple of years ago, leaving her in serious financial trouble. *But* she mysteriously received a large influx of cash into her accounts a few weeks ago. I'm working on locating the sender, but I don't know if I'll be able to. It's one of those anonymous overseas accounts, and it looks like it was funded through the dark web. As for the robberies in Sebastian's office back in Manhattan, the police don't have any leads. The only things taken were a couple of old laptops."

"Wow, Vince," Nick said with a relieved grin. "You're amazing."

"Given that I'm helping a rogue agent and a murder suspect, you realize that you're going to owe me drinks for the rest of your life?"

"Vince, my boy, when we're out of this mess, I'll buy you a bar," Nick returned.

"Seriously, though, Nick—take care," Vince said, his tone losing all traces of levity. "Briggs is like a dog without a bone; you know how he gets.

I'll do what I can to help, but the sooner you find out who's really behind all this . . ."

"We're working on it," Nick said. "Thanks again, Vince. I'll be in touch if we need anything else."

As Nick hung up, she thought about the revelation about Roberta. Someone had paid her for information, possibly about something Sebastian had told her. Some vital information about Cleopatra?

But why dispose of her? Adrian recalled their late-night visit to Roberta and guilt flared in her chest. If whoever paid her thought she was talking to the authorities, that would be a pretty good motivation for disposing of her.

"An abandoned farmhouse sounds like just the place you would bring a captive to," Nick said, forcing Adrian's thoughts back to the present. "But what if there's a group of men holding Sebastian?"

Her gaze again slid to Leonid. She and Nick had only barely managed to subdue him. If there were a group of such professionals, how could just the two of them take them on?

"I have an idea," Nick said after a brief stretch of tense silence. "But I warn you, it's not going to be fun."

∽

Monte Caminetto, Italy
8:38 A.M.

MONTE CAMINETTO WAS LOCATED ROUGHLY twenty kilometers north of Rome. Its name came from an ancient mountain referred to in Etruscan times. During the Roman era, it was dotted with spacious villas, which had now given way to a myriad of small farms and tourist-friendly bed-and-breakfasts.

As they drove through the region, Adrian wondered grimly if Sebastian was being held captive in one of these charming farmhouses.

Using Vince's directions, they parked on the side of a small dirt road one kilometer north of the farmhouse where they suspected Sebastian was being held.

Adrian turned to Nick, who looked anxious but determined. Julien looked shaken, his hands still gripping the steering wheel. They had switched drivers shortly after leaving Rome.

Nick's plan was risky, but they had no choice but to carry it out. There was only two of them who were going to approach the farmhouse, as they didn't know if Leonid, who was still unconscious in the backseat, could provide the leverage they needed to get Sebastian.

"Once we arrive at the farmhouse, we need to call the local police," Nick had proposed. Adrian had opened her mouth to protest, but Nick held up his hand to continue. "We can't risk entering the farmhouse on our own if there's a lot of them without significant backup. The local police will serve as our backup. Their arrival will definitely rattle Sebastian's abductors and they'll likely to attempt to flee with Sebastian. I know this is risky, but as they scatter, that's when we—or the police—can intercept him."

After considering his words for several moments, Adrian finally agreed. As risky as it was, police backup was their best shot at getting to Sebastian.

She turned to look at Julien. They'd given him another out, telling him he could leave them and go to the embassy for help, but he'd held firm and insisted that he wanted to help rescue Sebastian.

"Do you know how to use a gun?" Adrian asked him, reaching for the extra weapon they'd found on Leonid and confiscated. She didn't want to leave Julien here with a trained assassin, even one who was currently unconscious, without some kind of protection.

Julien shifted uncomfortably but nodded. "My dad took me shooting when I was younger."

Adrian handed it to him. "Don't hesitate to use this if necessary."

Nick placed the call, speaking in rapid Italian as he reported multiple gunshots at the farmhouse before abruptly hanging up.

"That should do it," he said, expelling a sigh. "We don't have much time. Ready?"

"I have no choice but to be," she replied.

With one last look at Julien, they readied their weapons—Nick's service weapon and Leonid's other gun—and got out of the car, darting in the farmhouse's direction.

8:42 A.M.

SEBASTIAN STUDIED the engraving on the ring, blood thrumming in his ears. He'd been using the digital microscope to examine it through the lens. Thankfully, his abductor had left him alone, giving him space to study it.

The delicately carved engraving consisted of a small sun and moon, which could stand for the names of Cleopatra's twins by Marc Antony. Cleopatra Selene for moon and Alexander Helios for sun. There was also a rendering of the goddess Isis, an important goddess of Cleopatra's day and a deity the queen associated herself with. The words were not written in Greek, or Latin, but in an Ethiopian script, one of the many languages he knew Cleopatra had spoken.

He translated the words for the dozenth time, a swelling of emotion rising in his chest.

He'd theorized for so long that there was more to Cleopatra's death than history told, and here was the proof of it staring right back at him. This was a message Cleopatra had intended for her children, he was certain of it, inscribed in a language few—if any—Romans would understand. It was almost as if Cleopatra was speaking directly to him through the ages, and for just a second, he forgot about the dire circumstances he was in.

But the door creaked open, forcing him back to the present and his precarious circumstances.

It wasn't his abductor who opened the door. Instead, it was a beautiful Egyptian woman with intense dark eyes that settled on him as she entered the room.

"Doctor Rossi," she said in near perfect English, giving him a wintry smile. "I'm Yara. It's nice to make your acquaintance. I didn't mean to startle you, but it looks like you've discovered something."

He stared at the woman, fear and fury battling for dominance. She was acting as if they'd just met at an academic conference, rather than as a captor addressing their prisoner. And he knew without a sliver of a doubt that this woman was behind his abduction; there was a cold ruthlessness beneath the veneer of her polite demeanor.

"Whatever you're about to say, Doctor Rossi," Yara said, her dark eyes flashing with danger, "I would advise you to keep it to yourself. Despite the circumstances, I'd like to keep things cordial. But I want to remind you that Mira and Celeste's fates are entirely in your hands right now."

The mention of his wife and daughter cooled his ire, and he swallowed hard, tamping down his fury.

"Nice to meet you," he said stiffly.

"That's better," Yara said calmly, stepping

forward and looking down at the ring. "Now tell me, what have you found?"

Before he could answer, the door swung open, and his abductor entered. Though he towered over the smaller woman, he seemed to quake in her presence.

"What is it, Markos?" Yara snapped.

"Security cameras have picked up two people—a man and a woman—approaching. It looks like they're armed."

CHAPTER 19

Monte Caminetto, Italy
8:45 A.M.

*A*drian and Nick crept toward the farmhouse, keeping low among the overgrown brush.

A swarthy man with dirty blond hair exited the front doors of the farmhouse, scanning the surroundings. He was armed.

She and Nick stilled, crouching down even lower.

The silence seemed to stretch for an eternity as she and Nick remained still. She could hear the guard speaking on his phone in both Arabic and Italian. His voice gradually grew louder.

He was approaching.

Adrian met Nick's eyes. Though she could tell he was just as alarmed as she was, he held himself rigid.

The guard's voice was getting even closer now, and Adrian knew they'd have no choice but to act. She reached for the weapon she'd tucked securely into the back of her pants. Nick did the same. And as they braced themselves to stand and fire—

The distant sound of sirens pierced the air, rapidly approaching.

Adrian heard the guard shout something she couldn't make out before his voice retreated. He was heading back to the farmhouse, clearly not wanting to deal with the local police.

It looked like Nick's plan was already working. And now that the guard was in retreat, it was their time to strike.

Adrenaline burst through Adrian as she and Nick exchanged another glance. This was their shot. If Sebastian was inside that farmhouse, they couldn't let him slip from their grasp.

"If they have Sebastian in there, they're likely going to get him out and take him to another location," Adrian said. "I'll take the back exit; you take the front."

Nick nodded his agreement, and they both raced forward.

JULIEN FROZE as he heard the sirens approaching, his hands tightening around the wheel.

In the back seat, Leonid was still slumped over, unconscious. Julien prayed he stayed that way. He also prayed that Nick and Adrian's plan worked, because there wasn't necessarily a backup plan.

While he'd been truthful about knowing how to use a gun, he eyed it warily as it rested on the passenger seat like a ticking time bomb. He hated the damn things and would rather not use it all. He honestly didn't know if he could, given the opportunity.

Adrian had told him, in no uncertain terms, to get himself to safety and not worry about them if it came to it. Julien knew his conscience wouldn't allow him to leave them behind, though he didn't know what else he could do to help them. He was hardly a trained law enforcement agent like Adrian and Nick.

He started the car, wanting to be prepared for Adrian and Nick's return, so focused on the sirens that he didn't notice movement in the backseat.

It wasn't until a dark awareness prickled at the back of his neck that he stiffened, his eyes meeting the infuriated gaze of Leonid's in the rearview mirror.

He hadn't been unconscious after all.

Before Julien could reach for the gun, the large man moved—quickly. He lifted his cuffed hands over the driver's seat, pressing his wrists around Julien's neck, strangling him. Panic seared Julien's insides; Leonid was cutting off his air; he was horrifically strong. Julien could barely move to dislodge him. Blackness seeped in the edges of his vision; he didn't have long before he'd lose consciousness altogether.

His survival instincts kicked in, and Julien used the last of his strength to bite down, hard, onto Leonid's exposed flesh, until he could feel flesh tearing and taste the coppery scent of his blood.

Leonid let out a roar, loosening his grip, and Julien slid out of his grasp, shoving open the car door and rolling out, but not before pushing the gear into drive, sending it lurching forward.

ADRIAN MOVED AROUND to the rear of the farmhouse, keeping low, continuing to use the cover of the surrounding brush and trees, clutching her gun tightly in her hands.

She stopped a couple of dozen yards away from the rear of the farmhouse behind the cluster of trees, going still as several figures hurried out, heading toward a waiting car. Her heart leapt into her throat at the sight of one of them.

It was Sebastian.

He was tied up and stumbling, dragged by a tall, burly man who looked eerily similar to Leonid, and followed by two women.

Knowing this was her only chance, Adrian darted forward, using the element of surprise to her advantage.

She shot the guard dragging Sebastian in the leg, causing him to drop to the ground with a pained cry. Sebastian and both of the women whirled toward her, startled, and before she could fire at either of the women, the smaller woman grabbed Sebastian and placed a gun to the side of his temple.

The driver of the waiting car emerged, training his gun on Adrian as she kept hers aimed at both of the women.

She met Sebastian's eyes. He was looking at her with a combination of hope, worry and fear. Other than a slightly bruised face, he seemed fine.

"Let him go!" she shouted.

The woman pressed the gun even harder into Sebastian's temple, causing fear to spike in Adrian. *She won't kill him,* she reassured herself. *She must need him alive.*

"His life means nothing to me," the woman said, as if reading her thoughts. "I won't hesitate to shoot him. Now, drop your weapon and kick it over to me."

Adrian hesitated.

"Adrian, don't do it," Sebastian cried. "*Bepēlusīyemi wisit'i ye'igizī'ābiḥēri sēti bēte-mek'idesi!*"

The woman struck Sebastian, sending him to his knees, and leveled her gun at his head. Panic flared in Adrian's belly; she couldn't risk it.

She dropped her gun and kicked it over to the woman.

"*Shukran,*" the woman said coolly.

Keeping the gun trained on Adrian, she

nodded to the second woman, who seemed to hesitate for a moment before taking Sebastian's arm and pushing him into the car, while the driver moved around the car to grab the burly man Adrian had shot and injured, hefting him into the car as well.

Once they were inside the car, the woman gave Adrian a cold smile, raised her gun, and fired.

CHAPTER 20

Monte Caminetto, Italy
Five Minutes Ago

Nick's instincts were on sharp alert as he made his way to the entrance of the farmhouse in a low crouch, his hands on his gun, his gaze laser focused on the entrance of the farmhouse. The sirens were still distant but getting closer. It wouldn't be long before the police arrived.

Readying his weapon, he straightened, making his way to the door—when it swung open. The dirty blond guard he and Adrian had seen before emerged, clutching a bag, freezing at the sight of Nick.

Nick reacted first. He moved quickly, darting forward, kicking out at the man's knees to send him tumbling to the ground before he could reach for his own weapon.

Nick raised his gun, but the son of a bitch was

fast, dodging him to roll away, reaching for his gun and raising it to aim—

Nick cursed and knocked the gun out of the guard's hand, and as he scrambled for it, Nick slammed the barrel of his gun on the back of the man's skull with all of his strength. The guard slumped forward, his body going slack.

Nick pocketed the guard's weapon, straightening as he heard a gunshot fire out. He froze, fear like he'd never known coursing through his veins like ice.

Adrian.

Moving as fast as his legs would carry him, he raced around to the rear of the farmhouse. Relief flooded him as he saw Adrian tucked securely behind a tree as a car sped off, its tires squealing.

"Adrian!" he shouted.

He raced toward her as she stumbled to her feet. He pulled her into his arms, and he allowed his relief to settle over him, quelling his panic.

"The woman who abducted Sebastian—she fired at me, but I dodged it," she said, when they broke apart. "They had Sebastian. And I lost him."

She gritted her teeth and cursed, kicking the tree. Nick's gut clenched, but the sirens were almost upon them; there was no time to comfort her now.

"I'm sorry, Adrian. But we need to find Julien and get the hell out of here."

Sacrofano, Italy
9:15 A.M.

ADRIAN, Julien, and Nick sat in silence as their cab made its way down the *strada provinciale* toward the village of Sacrofano, only a few kilometers north of Monte Caminetto.

Adrian and Nick had headed east on foot to give the farmhouse some distance before the police arrived. They'd come upon Julien walking south in the direction away from where he'd parked.

He'd told them about Leonid's escape, looking shame-faced, though she and Nick had assured him what he'd done was brave. Leonid could have easily killed him.

They'd continued to head away from the farm-house on foot. Once they were a safe distance away, Julien had called for a cab. An archaeologist friend of his had an apartment in Sacrofano. He was out of town and Julien had access to it. There, they could regroup and figure out what to do next.

Adrian leaned back in her seat, frustration and despair colliding within her. She had been so close yet had still failed to rescue Sebastian. And she was flummoxed over what he had shouted at her before the woman had shoved him into the car.

"*Bepēlusīyemi wisit'i ye'igizī'ābiḥēri sēti bēte-mek'idesi!*"

She repeated the strange words in her mind, words she had mostly committed to memory. Adrian spoke seven languages, and the words didn't belong to any language she was familiar with, but by the structure and cadence she knew they belonged to the Afro-Asiatic language family, specifically the Semitic branch.

Once they got to Sacrofano, she needed to take the time to break the words down phonetically before attempting to translate them.

What were you trying to tell me, Sebastian?

~

Monte Caminetto, Italy
9:20 A.M.

LEONID SPED down the road out of Monte Caminetto, gritting his teeth in pain at the injury that *zasranec* had given him. He should have killed the bastard, but given that police sirens had been approaching, he'd focused instead on getting out of there.

As he'd sped away, he'd picked up one of Yara's hired guards, who was injured and limping away from the farmhouse. Not out of the goodness of his heart; he needed his phone, and the guard had helped free him of his cuffs.

The guard now sat in the backseat, still rubbing his temple in pain. He'd told him the male FBI agent had knocked him out with his gun, and that Yara and the others had fled.

Keeping one eye on the road, Leonid dialed Yara.

"How did they find us?" she hissed by greeting.

"I don't know," he lied. He knew Yara would eventually find out about his abduction and his cell phone being traced—she had ways of finding such things out—but he wasn't going to admit it. He was embarrassed enough that West and Harper had managed to both subdue him and use him to get to Yara's hideout.

"I was—" he began.

"None of that matters now," she interrupted. "Meet me at the airport. We know where the treasure is."

He froze, his pulse racing.

"I'll explain when you arrive," she continued, and her voice softened. "I'm glad you are safe, my *volk.*"

She's manipulating you, he reminded himself. Still, he felt himself softening.

He ended the call, closing his eyes, and forcing himself to harden his heart again. He couldn't let his lust for Yara sway him from his ultimate goal.

With that in mind, he pulled over to send a quick text, ignoring the guard's confused utter of protest in the back seat.

Yara knows where the treasure is. When do we act? he typed.

The response came almost instantly.

We need to confirm location of treasure.
Once it's in hand, we act immediately.

CHAPTER 21

Twenty-Five Kilometers South of Monte Caminetto, Italy

9:32 A.M.

Sebastian's body hummed with pain, still smarting from the blows that Yara had rained down upon him with Adrian's gun. He huddled in his seat as the car hurtled down the A90 motorway toward Leonardo da Vinci International Airport.

For a petite woman, Yara possessed great strength, and she'd been furious with him for shouting out to Adrian.

Adrian. At the sight of her, he'd never felt such combined fear and relief at once in his life. He should have known that his former student turned loyal friend would be right on his trail once she'd learned he was missing. Terror had torn through him when he saw Yara fire at her, but her training must have kicked in, because she had evaded the shot and darted away through the cluster of trees behind her.

To his relief, Yara hadn't pursued her, muttering a curse before entering the car and ordering the driver to go, as those distant sirens drew closer and closer.

The message he'd shouted to Adrian was one he hoped she could decode. It was the only way Adrian could know where Yara was taking him next. He'd purposefully used a language he knew his abductors would likely not understand.

As they'd sped away from the farmhouse, Yara had pressed a pistol to his head and demanded to know what he'd told Adrian, promising to execute Mira and Celeste if he didn't tell her the truth.

He'd forced the words past his lips, telling Yara what she wanted to know, feeling sick at the hungry look in her eyes as he'd told her what he'd learned from the inscription on the ring.

Sebastian closed his eyes, dread seizing him at the thought of their destination. He felt not even a sliver of excitement at the prospect of finding Cleopatra's lost treasure. Once it was found, Yara and her cronies would have no use for him.

Please, Adrian, he prayed silently, *please get there before we do*.

Sacrofano, Italy

10:02 A.M.

SACROFANO WAS an ancient commune that had been around since the time of the Etruscans; it was now a quaint village that served as a respite for tourists and locals wanting to escape the hubbub of Rome. Compared to the bustling Rome, it was a haven filled with rolling green hills dotted by patches of trees, red-tiled homes and old medieval buildings.

The apartment Julien took them to in Sacrofano was a spacious loft on the top floor of one such medieval building.

Adrian, Julien and Nick now sat in the living room, eating Caprese sandwiches that Julien had bought for them from a corner store. She'd relayed Sebastian's cryptic message to Nick and Julien, but they were also flummoxed.

Think, Adrian. She set down her sandwich, closing her eyes. Sebastian would often use riddles and wordplay in both his classes and in his leisure time. But in that moment of panic and fear, Sebastian would be much more straightforward.

She thought of a game she liked to play with her freshman students. It was similar to a game she'd played with her father when she was a child. He'd draw a large tree and hang different words from various branches of the tree, giving her a point when she successfully guessed which language family the word belonged to. Whenever her students were trying to detect the language of a word that was unfamiliar to them, she had them start by drawing a tree and identify the language branch.

"From the sound structure and pattern of the words Sebastian spoke, the language is Semitic. Cleopatra spoke nine languages: Greek, Latin, Parthian, Median, Arabic, Egyptian . . ."

"Ethiopian, Syriac, and Hebrew," Julien finished.

"OK. So, of those languages, it's likely Ethiopian, Hebrew, or Syriac. It's not Hebrew. That leaves us with Ethiopian—which is now called Amharic—or Syriac."

"This is where technology comes in," Julien said with a grin, taking out his phone and handing it to her. There was a language translation application already open. They'd already tried using it, but without knowing the exact language, the words she'd spoken into it had come out as gibberish. "Let's try this again, shall we?"

Adrian chose Amharic as the source language, and spoke Sebastian's words into the app, slowly and clearly. She had to repeat them several times until finally, a match came back.

Temple of the Woman God in Pelusium

CHAPTER 22

Embassy of the United States - FBI Offices
Rome, Italy
10:05 A.M.

"Vince got back to us with that information you wanted about Julien Caron. He's an archaeologist—big with the millennials. My kid follows him on YouTube," Agent Andrews told Briggs as they made their way through the embassy. "His father is a billionaire, a member of this old banking family in France. But Caron chose to go into his mother's field of archaeology instead, using his money to fund his research."

Briggs was only half listening.

After not finding any traces of Julien Caron, Nick, or West, they had returned to the embassy to regroup, and frustration still surged through him. He knew that his boss wanted an update call; he was not looking forward to telling him about yet another setback.

"And get this," Andrews continued, "he's an expert on Ptolemaic Egypt."

Briggs halted in his tracks. This answered his question about why they'd sought Julien Caron, and it solidified his theory that all of this had to do with the stolen Cleopatra artifacts. But how?

"Agent Briggs."

He looked up as his harried assistant approached, interrupting his train of thought. "Sebastian Rossi's wife is here. She's waiting in your office—she insisted on waiting there."

Briggs stiffened but gave him a nod, turning to Andrews. "Keep me updated," he said, making his way to his office.

Mira Rossi, an attractive blond woman in her fifties, stood just inside his office, waiting for him. She didn't smile as Briggs greeted her; the look she gave him was downright frosty.

"I overheard some of your agents. Is Adrian West really a suspect for Roberta Fields' murder and my husband's disappearance?" she demanded.

Briggs silently cursed his agents for their lack of protocol. Mira shouldn't have heard any of that.

"We're investigating persons of interest," Briggs said, hedging. "We— "

"If you're looking into Adrian West, you're wasting your time," Mira interrupted. "Adrian is like a daughter to Sebastian. After what happened to her own father, he's the only father figure she has."

"Mrs. Rossi, I assure you we are doing everything we— "

"Not if you're investigating Adrian," she insisted. "Someone robbed our apartment back in New York. This all has to do with the artifacts. That's what you should focus on."

He stiffened. He didn't know about this burglary.

"When did this happen?"

"I just found out about it. Adrian advised me to check to see if anyone had burgled us, and I did," Mira replied.

"I'll have someone look into that," he said, perturbed. This was more sprawling than he'd thought. He schooled his features into one of professional neutrality, returning his focus back to Mira. "And I appreciate your input, but we're doing everything we can to find your husband. We'll keep you informed every step of the way. You can call me at any time."

He took a business card from his desk and handed it to her. It was a dismissal, and they both knew it. Mira stiffened, and for a moment he thought she would refuse it, but she took his card and stalked from the office.

He watched her go, frowning. As annoyed as he was, he knew she was right about one thing. This was all related to the artifacts.

And deep down, he was beginning to have

niggling doubts about exactly what Adrian West's role was in all of this.

≈

Sacrofano, Italy
10:07 A.M.

"TEMPLE of the Woman God in Pelusium?" Nick said, his eyebrows knitted together in a confused frown as he read the translated words over Adrian's shoulder. "Where's Pelusium?"

"Egypt," Adrian said. "Pelusium has gone by many names; the ancient Egyptians called it Sent and Per-Amun. The Greeks called it Pelouison—from their word for mud, *pelos*. Now it goes by the name of Tell-al-Farama. It was an important fortress town in antiquity, along what was once ancient Egypt's military road called 'the great Horus route' after the Egyptian sky god. It protected Egypt from foreign invaders dating back to the time of the pharaohs."

"Indeed," Julien said, looking impressed by Adrian's knowledge. She just gave him a wan smile. Given how important Pelusium was in the ancient world, she'd learned much about it from Sebastian himself.

"When Alexander the Great conquered Egypt, it was one of the first places he entered and set up a garrison there," Julien continued. "It was also of great importance to the Ptolemies. The city had once been lost and then restored to her ancestor Ptolemy Philometor in battle. Marc Antony, Cleopatra's lover, had even once made himself leader of Pelusium after defeating the Egyptian army there on behalf of her father, Auletes. Cleopatra herself went there as a young, exiled queen and led an army of mercenaries against her brother to take back her throne. Besides being a fortress city, it was a bustling trading post," he added. "It fell in the seventh century to the invading Persians and was eventually abandoned by the Middle Ages."

"Now it's an archaeological site," Adrian said, looking up at Nick. "It's been under excavations since the early twentieth century. They're still discovering things there to this day."

"I've had several digs there. They're indeed still making discoveries like Roman baths, amphitheaters, even what used to be major streets of the ancient city," Julien said, nodding in agreement. "They're using some pretty interesting technology —including geophysical mapping—to help uncover ruins. But there's still only a small portion of Pelusium excavated."

There was a brief, momentous silence at his words . . . and their meaning.

"So, there could be a treasure there, still waiting to be discovered," Nick said slowly. "I'm going to assume there are many temples at this site. How do we know which one to go to?"

"Well, the Woman God can be translated to

'goddess'," Adrian said.

"OK, which goddess? Weren't there a bunch worshipped in Cleopatra's day?" Nick asked.

"There were," Julien said. "But there was no goddess more important to Cleopatra than the goddess Isis. She was the consort of the god Osiris and popular in both Egypt and Rome; there was even a religious festival in Rome dedicated to her: the *Navigium Isidis,* which can be translated as the vessel of Isis. And many of Cleopatra's female ancestors also identified with Isis. She was—and still is by some—considered the essence of feminine divinity."

Adrian nodded her agreement. It seemed doubtful that the temple they were seeking would be dedicated to any other goddess but Isis.

"All right," Nick said, frowning. "So we go to what used to be Pelusium, locate this temple, and then what? We just start digging?"

"Even I don't have the resources to do something like that. Fortunately, there's been a recent set of excavations done on an old church from the first century CE. This church was built over an older temple that was active during the time of Cleopatra. It's believed to be a temple dedicated to Isis."

"If it's already been excavated, then there's no way they missed a treasure," Adrian said, confused by Julien's palpable excitement.

"Or is there?" Julien pressed. "Sebastian clearly found something among the Cleopatra artifacts that pointed to Pelusium."

Adrian considered this. He could be right. Why else would Sebastian tell her about the temple of the goddess in Pelusium? That could only mean that something had pointed him in that direction, and it was probably where his abductor was taking him next.

"Where would these excavated items go?" Adrian asked.

"The Museum of Antiquities in El Qantara. I know a contact of Sebastian's who works there. I can ask her if I can look at them—I'll just have to think of some cover story."

Adrian knew that a treasure being hidden among excavated items in a small museum was unlikely, but there could very well be a clue leading to its actual location.

In any case, she was becoming increasingly convinced that this treasure was in Egypt. And wherever the treasure was, that's where Sebastian's abductors would take him.

"It looks like we need to go to Egypt," she said.

But how could they get there, now that she and Nick were on the run? There was no doubt the FBI had already sent out an alert to the airlines.

Julien met her gaze and grinned. "Well, it's a good thing I have access to a private plane, courtesy of dear old Dad."

Nick cocked a brow, turning to look at Adrian. "I'm starting to think that bringing Mr. Moneybags along for the ride was a good idea."

CHAPTER 23

Port Said, Egypt
1:45 P.M.

Yara looked out at the desolate stretch of road that led from Port Said to the archeological site of Pelusium as her driver maneuvered down it.

How she hated this country. If it weren't for its significant history and being the residence of the great Cleopatra, she would never come back here. She had left years ago, broken, desperate and alone, before Dalal had rescued her and she'd come to learn her true purpose.

Her gaze swiveled to the professor, who sat huddled opposite her, his face still bruised. Sebastian didn't know she'd been easy on him; she could have had Leonid beat him for his defiance.

Annoyance skittered through her as she glanced over at Leonid, who sat in the front next to the driver. She'd had to feign relief at seeing him when he'd met her at the airport, though she was infuriated that he'd allowed himself to get captured.

But she didn't have time to deal with Leonid now; she was on the verge of obtaining Cleopatra's treasure. If she wasn't, there would be severe consequences for him.

She found herself wishing that Leonid had been shot instead of Markos, whom West had shot before they'd fled the farmhouse. Markos was currently being tended to by a trusted doctor outside of Rome. Despite his injured leg, he'd wanted to come.

"I can help—my leg is fine," he'd insisted.

"I need you healed," Yara had firmly replied.

"I'll be on the next flight over," he'd said, giving her a firm look that wasn't to be argued with.

I should have taken Markos to my bed instead of Leonid, she thought bitterly. He'd been of far more use to her, while Leonid had just led West right to them.

Keeping West alive had been a good idea at first, giving her former colleagues a bad guy to focus on while Yara sought the treasure. But now West was becoming a nuisance.

If Yara encountered West again, she would not survive.

Currently, Yara, Sebastian and her associates—Fairuza, Leonid, her driver, and two additional guards who'd replaced the ones injured back in Italy, were heading to the archeological site that had once been the great border fortress town of Pelusium. Their destination was the partially excavated ruins of a church that had been built over a temple of Isis from Cleopatra's time.

Her contacts had learned there was a dig that was occurring there today that wouldn't be complete until just before sunset, which was also around the time the last of the tourists left. Yara's team, sourced from trusted members of the Daughters, wouldn't be able to start digging at the site until later. Though she was annoyed at the inconvenience of having to wait, eager anticipation coursed through her.

She was so close.

Yara opened her eyes to find Sebastian glaring at her with undisguised hatred. He quickly looked away when Yara met his eyes, but she merely smiled.

"I know it doesn't seem this way, but I have great respect for you, Professor."

Sebastian glowered at her, then looked down at his handcuffed hands. "It doesn't seem like it."

Yara removed the handcuff key from her pocket and leaned forward, not missing Sebastian's flinch as she unlocked his handcuffs.

"There is a legend among my family that we're descended from Cleopatra through ties with Zenobia, another great ancient queen," she said. "I like to think of Cleopatra's blood running through my veins."

"Is that why you're doing this?" Sebastian asked. "Because you believe you're her heir?"

Yara laughed. "No, I'm not as self-serving as that. I want the treasure for a greater good. A greater purpose. I think Cleopatra would be proud."

The professor's expression showed that he doubted that very much, but Yara didn't care. "When I have the treasure in my hands, there will be a new world order," she proclaimed.

Sebastian stilled, and she took great pleasure in the fear that shone in his eyes. "What do you mean?"

Yara's smile widened. Sebastian would be dead soon; there was no risk in him telling anyone. And she enjoyed speaking of the Daughters' goals out loud.

"My organization will overthrow tyranny —*male* tyranny," she specified.

While there was no longer a Roman Empire, there were plenty of modern day patriarchal empires that oppressed women, from the so-called progressive West to the Middle East, the former turning a blind eye to the latter's treatment of women because of its greed over the natural resources of the Middle East.

The Daughters' funding had been lacking in recent years due to a declining membership. In order to carry out their lofty goals, they needed more funding. Lots of it.

While they intended to preserve a small

portion of the treasure for their archives, the majority of it they intended to sell on the black market, bringing in the funding they needed to carry out their plans. They already had several buyers waiting, thanks to contacts Dalal had introduced her to before her death.

With the money from the sale of the treasure, the Daughters intended to purchase weapons to carry out a series of attacks on the most powerful governments of the Middle East, bringing them to their proverbial knees, installing mostly female members of the Daughters as leaders amid the chaos.

Under the leadership of the Daughters, they intended to withhold their resources from the West, cutting off diplomatic ties many countries in the region had to the West. They also intended to raise the position of women in society and to wreak vengeance on the male leadership for their continued subjugation.

But they did not limit their sights to just the Middle East. They also had planned attacks on governments of the West, particularly the United States, taking their revenge for its continual plundering of their region's resources, leaving the vulnerable—particularity women—suffering in their wake.

Once they had funding, it would only be a matter of weeks before carrying out the attacks. The plans were already in place.

She could recall her disbelief when Dalal first

told her of these ultimate goals, but Dalal had only smiled and told her that many powerful governments, especially the United States, had overthrown governments in weaker countries and then installed their own puppet leaders. It was hardly anything new.

"Yes, there will be innocents hurt in the crossfire, but it's a necessary sacrifice, and it will fulfill the promise of Cleopatra's legacy," Dalal had said.

Now Yara studied Sebastian, giving him a cool smile. "Just know that you have helped change the world . . . for the better."

At her words, his skin grew pale and fear tightened his features.

She understood his fear. Change could be a frightening thing. Yet it was necessary.

And once she had the treasure, it was change she could enact.

CHAPTER 24

Port Said, Egypt
3:47 P.M.

During the three-hour plane ride from Rome, Adrian, Nick and Julien prepared their plan for what they'd do when they reached El Qantara.

Needing some levity after this intense planning session, Adrian and Nick swapped stories of their time working together at the bureau for Julien, with Nick doing his best to make them both laugh.

Adrian was trying to keep her mind off worrying about Sebastian, glad that Nick was trying to provide them all with some lightness before they landed in Egypt. By the time the pilot announced they were beginning their final descent, Adrian and Julien were laughing over a story Nick was telling them about an art theft case he'd worked on in Montreal, only to learn that the precious seventeenth-century painting hadn't been stolen at all; its absentminded owner had simply forgotten he'd stored it in his cellar.

As their private plane landed at the tiny airport in Port Said, memories swept over Adrian. She had traveled to Egypt several times before. Once as a kid with her parents, one other time as a federal agent attending a counterterrorism conference, and then as an academic attending a linguistics conference.

But it was this first memory she clung to, the memory of sitting on her father's shoulders as they approached the Great Pyramid. *This was built thousands of years ago, honey*, he'd told her, as she'd taken it in with awe. It was this trip to Egypt as a child that had begun her fascination with the ancient past and eventually led to her career in academia after her stint with the FBI.

Once they landed and Julien made a quick call to a contact of his, they made their way to a car, a sleek and modern Mercedes Benz, that was waiting for them.

Julien took the wheel, driving them the hour-long distance to El Qantara, a small, modern city straddling the two sides of the Suez Canal. During the drive, Adrian and Nick checked their weapons; they needed to be prepared in case Sebastian's abductors were already at the museum in El Qantara. They already had a plan; the weapons were a backup she hoped they wouldn't have to use. Her nerves were on edge at the thought. If she had the chance to rescue Sebastian a second time, she wouldn't fail.

She couldn't.

The Museum of Antiquities was located in the central part of the city, and Adrian ordered Julien to park across the street so that she and Nick could survey it for danger. The parking lot was empty except for one car that Julien identified as belonging to his contact. Still, they made Julien walk several yards behind them, keeping their guns easily reachable in case of an ambush.

As they approached, the only person who emerged from the museum was Julien's contact, a middle-aged woman by the name of Karima. She looked baffled by their cautious approach.

"Are you the only one here?" Adrian asked sharply after Julien made introductions.

"Y-yes. We closed an hour ago," Karima stammered. Her startled gaze flew to Julien. "Julien, what's going on?"

Julien hesitated. He'd informed Karima he needed to look at the artifacts excavated from Pelusium because of a last-minute talk he was giving on the goddess Isis at Cairo University; they had held off on telling her too much over the phone.

"I'll tell you inside," he said finally.

Karima studied him for a long moment before ushering them inside. The museum was even smaller than it appeared from the outside, comprising three rooms filled with Egyptian artifacts.

Once they were all inside, Karima closed the door, crossed her arms, and faced Julien.

"Well?" she asked.

"This is about the stolen artifacts from Rome, the ones that belong to Cleopatra's daughter," Julien said. "We think that the artifacts here may lead to them."

It was a half-truth, no mention of a treasure, which relieved Adrian. Julien told them he trusted Karima, but they could never be too careful.

At his words, Karima's eyes widened in surprise, her gaze going to Adrian and Nick.

"I'm Agent Nick Harper from the Federal Bureau of Investigation out of the States," Nick said, answering her silent question. "And this is my colleague, Adrian West. We just want to take a quick look at the artifacts and then we'll be out of your way."

Karima still looked stunned, but she nodded. She turned and led them through the rooms to an even smaller back room.

"I doubt you'll find anything significant," Karima said as she unlocked the door. "A team of archaeologists have already thoroughly examined them."

She led them inside, where a dozen artifacts were carefully laid out on a long table.

"As you requested, these are all from the latest excavation at the Pelusium site."

Julien sat down at the table as Karima handed

him a pair of gloves. Adrian and Nick hovered behind him, taking it in.

The artifacts laid out on the table included a bronze censer, used for burning incense in temples, a clay seal, which would have been used to seal the door of a shrine, and a fragment of a sandstone stela, which depicted Egyptians worshipping Isis, and a tiny gypsum figurine of the goddess herself, carved in intricate detail.

"What exactly are we looking for?" Nick asked as Julien examined each artifact.

"Anything out of the ordinary. Any hint that there's a message Cleopatra or her followers inscribed, pointing to a different location," Julien said, lifting up the gypsum figurine and studying it closely. "Something so embedded a team of archaeologists could have missed it."

"A—message?" Karima gasped. "Julien, what's going on?"

Julien looked at Adrian and Nick. Adrian subtly shook her head; she didn't want to risk putting anyone else in danger by telling them about the treasure.

"I can't tell you anymore for now. I'm sorry," Julien said.

Karima stiffened, and Adrian braced herself for protest. Instead, Karima gave him a jerky nod.

"Let me get you a digital microscope. It's in my office," she said, turning to leave the room.

"We might as well tell her," Julien grumbled. "She might be able to help us."

Adrian considered this, meeting Nick's gaze. He lifted a shoulder in a shrug. "He's right. And at the moment, we need all the help we can get."

Adrian heaved a sigh. Maybe they were right. She just prayed they weren't putting the poor woman in danger.

The door swung open behind them, and Adrian turned, on the verge of telling Karima they could use her help . . . but the words died on her lips.

Karima stood in the doorway, a pistol in her hand, leveling it right at them. Her expression was stony, devoid of anything but icy determination.

Julien gasped, getting to his feet. "Karima, what are you—"

"Sit back down," she said, her voice razor sharp. "We'll have visitors soon. It will be much easier for you if you tell me what you're really looking for."

CHAPTER 25

El Qantara, Egypt
5:47 P.M.

read coiled around Sebastian's spine as their SUV arrived at a small museum. If Adrian was here with no backup, she stood little chance against Yara and her men. *I should have somehow bought her more time,* he thought, guilt filling him.

At the archeological site in Pelusium, Yara's team had begun to dig at the location, the ruins of the temple dedicated to Isis. He thought of the inscription on the amethyst ring, carved beneath the rendering of the goddess Isis, written in Amharic. *Fourth of the great ports.* Alexandria, Cleopatra's city, was only one of several large ports in her day. There were four: Alexandria, Rosietta, Damietta, and Pelusium. From west to east, Pelusium was the fourth of the great ports.

He'd desperately not wanted to tell Yara of his conjecture, but he'd had no choice. He felt divided. If he was wrong, he'd put his wife and daughter in harm's way. Yet if there was indeed a treasure here, Yara would have no incentive to keep him alive.

Would she shoot him and leave him for dead? Buried in a meaningless stretch of Egyptian desert, never to see his wife and daughter again?

Panic made his throat close, and he pushed past it. No. He was determined to survive this.

It was while he was deep in his rumination that Yara received a phone call and stepped away to take it. When she ended the call, she approached Sebastian and gestured to one of her men, who punched him in the abdomen, sending him to his knees, wheezing in pain.

"What else did you tell Adrian West?" Yara hissed.

"Exactly what I told you!" he cried. "I wouldn't put my family's lives at risk—I told her what I told you!"

Yara glared at him for a few tense moments before nodding to her driver. Sebastian braced himself for more blows, but the man had dragged him from the ground and back to the car. They promptly left the site in Pelusium, heading to El Qantara. Sebastian huddled in the backseat during the entire drive, not knowing where they were going, terror gripping him.

Now he eyed the museum with unease as they approached. A contact of his worked here, Karima.

Fear flooded him; he didn't want her to get involved in this. Adrian must have discovered something here, and whoever she was with had betrayed her to Yara. He wished he could warn her, but at the moment, he was helpless.

As Yara and her men exited the car, Fairuza took him firmly by the arm as they trailed the others inside.

"Spread out," Yara ordered her men in Arabic once they entered the empty museum.

They all froze when they heard a muffled cry. Yara hurried forward, following the sound to the closed door of a back room. One of her men took out his weapon and shoved open the door.

Inside, Karima was seated on the ground, her hands and feet bound with tape.

"I-I tried to get information out of them, but they escaped," Karima said, her eyes filling with tears.

Horror filled Sebastian as he took in Karima, who was only focused on Yara. She was working with Yara?

"Outside!" Yara shouted, and her men darted toward the rear exit.

Fairuza tightened her grip on Sebastian's arm, dragging him toward the rear exit after the others.

Outside, Yara's men shouted frantically to each other in Arabic as they rounded the building to the front. "There they are! They're crossing!"

Still clutching his arm, Fairuza yanked Sebastian around to the front of the building. There, he glimpsed Adrian with two men, one of whom he recognized as Julien Caron, as they darted inside a parked car across the road from the museum. Yara and her men were racing toward them as the car roared to life.

Sebastian's heart rate quickened. Fairuza, focused on the chaos across the road, had loosened her grip on his arm.

He knew that if he stayed with these people, they would kill him. In that moment, he made a decision, one that he prayed wouldn't be fatal.

Sebastian elbowed Fairuza in the ribs, causing her to completely loosen her grip, and moving as fast as his legs would carry him, he raced across the road.

Directly toward Adrian's car.

ADRIAN SWERVED out of their parking spot to turn right. In the passenger seat, Nick took out his gun as Yara's men rushed toward them, lifting their own weapons to fire.

As Adrian yanked the car to the right, nearly careening into an oncoming car, the headlights lit up a familiar figure that was racing right toward them.

Adrian stilled. It was Sebastian.

Yara's men shouted, redirecting their attention to Sebastian.

She didn't have much time.

Adrian reacted fast, swerving directly toward the men and making them scatter. Nick, who had also spotted Sebastian, opened the passenger side door.

"Get in!" he shouted. Sebastian darted toward them, and Nick yanked him inside, slamming the door shut, just as bullets ricocheted off the car—

Adrian pressed her foot down on the accelerator, racing away from the museum and Yara's men, but she could already see them rushing toward their SUVs to pursue them.

Heart pounding, her gaze found Sebastian's in the rearview mirror as Julien helped him into the backseat. Though he looked pale and shaken, he gave Adrian a wavering smile.

"Took you long enough," he quipped, "and I still had to take matters into my own hands."

Relief spread through her as she returned his smile, but it was short-lived. It was only a matter of time before Yara and her men caught up to them.

"We're not out of the woods yet," she said, her tone grim. "Buckle up and stay low. Both of you."

Sebastian and Julien obliged, sinking down low in their seats. Nick gripped his weapon, his gaze scanning both the rearview and side mirrors. Adrian couldn't see Yara and her men, but she knew they could catch up to them at any moment.

Just as she had the thought, Nick shouted her name, and she followed his gaze. A few cars behind them, two black SUVs were bearing down on them.

Yara's men. And they were gaining on them —fast.

Adrian's pulse raced, her gaze focused on the road ahead. It was time to execute the plan she'd concocted on the plane during the flight here.

Their Hail Mary.

"Hold on everyone," she shouted, and floored the gas.

CHAPTER 26

El Qantara, Egypt
6:32 P.M.

Adrian sped toward the outskirts of El Qantara, weaving in and out of traffic, her gaze continually straying to the rearview mirror as Julien directed her where to go.

Their pursuers were still a few cars behind them; Adrian weaved the car around the vehicles blocking them up ahead, ignoring the curses and shouts at her in Arabic.

"Hold tight!" she shouted.

She reached the main road leading out of the city and could just make out the signs indicating the direction toward Cairo in Arabic. She trained her eyes on the rearview mirror as she made an abrupt left, turning onto a side road that made a U-turn back into El Qantara, taking advantage of a passing large four-wheeler truck to block them from their pursuers.

In the backseat, she could feel Sebastian's puzzled gaze on her back, likely wondering why the hell they were turning to head back into the city. But she kept her focus on the road, taking smaller side streets as she ventured back into El Qantara, periodically checking the rearview to make certain they weren't being followed.

"Why are we going back?" Sebastian demanded.

"I'll explain in a second," she said, keeping her gaze trained on the road. "Julien, am I going the right way?"

"Keep going straight," Julien said, sitting up and peering around cautiously.

Adrian nodded, praying that this worked, and that they weren't heading into a trap.

Back on the plane, they'd determined that they didn't want to risk making the same mistakes they'd had at the farmhouse in Italy, so they'd prepared for their possible getaway.

"Do you know anyone in El Qantara who can help us?" Adrian had asked Julien. "Preferably someone who doesn't know your contact at the museum, in case she's compromised."

Julien told them about a local driver he used whenever he was in the area; he'd contacted him before they'd left the airport in Port Said, proposing an exchange. A better car and money if he left his car in a tucked away alley in El Qantara for a block of time. The Mercedes they'd taken from the airport back in Port Said belonged to his father; Julien told them he wouldn't miss it.

"Rich people," Nick muttered, shaking his head in both amusement and awe.

As Adrian turned onto another side street that led to an alley at Julien's direction, relief washed over her when she saw that Julien's contact had paid off. There was a small, beat-up Toyota waiting for them.

"We need to move fast," she said, pulling over to park behind the car.

Adrian and Nick kept watch as Sebastian and Julien made their way into the Toyota, leaving their newer car behind for whom Adrian assumed would be a very grateful driver.

It was only after Julien took the wheel and they had safely made their way out of the city with no sign of their pursuers that the tension dissolved from Adrian's belly. They had escaped danger —for now.

As they made their way toward Cairo, Sebastian told them everything that happened to him since his abduction in Rome. Her gut tightened at the realization of how easily things could have gone wrong . . . how easily Sebastian could have been killed.

"I'm all right now, thanks to you," he said gently, seeming to note the trepidation in her expression. "I need to make sure my wife and daughter are safe—they've been under surveillance by my abductor."

"I'll send a message to my contact Vince. He can alert the higher ups at the bureau to get some protection to your family," Nick said, taking out his phone.

Sebastian noded, looking visibly relieved, before turning back to Adrian. "And there's more I need to tell you. About Yara, the woman who abducted me, and what she plans to do."

"I assume find the treasure and become a very wealthy woman?" Julien quipped.

"I wish," Sebastian said grimly.

As Sebastian told them about the Daughters of Cleopatra and Yara's plans for the treasure once it was found, fear and dread coiled around her. Adrian closed her eyes, taking a shuddering breath. She shouldn't have been surprised; something deep down had told her that this was more than just a simple theft.

"Well then, it's up to us to stop them," Adrian said, determination flaring to life within her. She turned to Julien. "I need to use your phone."

Embassy of the United States - FBI Offices
Rome, Italy
6:50 P.M.

"AGENT BRIGGS," the voice on the other end of the line said. "This is Adrian West. I believe you've been looking for me.

Briggs froze at the sound of Adrian's voice on the line. He stood and waved frantically to Andrews and Vince through the open door of his office, gesturing for a trace.

The call couldn't have come at a more perfect time. He'd just learned that Julien Caron had made use of his private plane and landed at a small airport in Port Said, Egypt. They were trying to determine exactly where they had gone from there, coordinating with the FBI's office in Cairo, but that was becoming a red-tape nightmare, and no information had been forthcoming.

"Adrian," he said, trying to keep his voice steady, "it's good to hear from you."

"I'm calling you with Sebastian Rossi at my side. The actual murderers of Roberta Fields are the ones who abducted him. They're the ones you should be looking for."

He listened, stunned and increasingly chilled, as Adrian told him what she had discovered, even putting Sebastian on the line to confirm her story and to request protection for his family. He gave him two names to work with: Yara and Leonid.

"As you can see, I'm not the person you need to be focused on," Adrian said, returning to the line. "We need to be working together on this."

"Agreed," Briggs said, "which is why I just want to talk to—"

"We'll be in touch."

"Adrian, wait—"

She had already hung up. Briggs stood in silence for a moment, reeling at all she had told him.

"We need eyes on Sebastian Rossi's wife and daughter. Put a couple of agents on them for protection. And get our field office in Cairo on the phone," he said, looking up at Andrews. "I also want a background and criminal search on the names Sebastian gave us. We need to be on the next flight to Egypt."

CHAPTER 27

Desert on the Outskirts of El Qantara, Egypt
7:02 P.M.

ara paced next to the parked SUV, fury pumping through her veins. Even though they'd been right on West's tail, they'd lost her . . . and Sebastian.

She'd ordered her men to search the city and the surrounding roads, and to find out everything they could about Julien Caron, the man her contact Karima had told her about. Right now, it was the best way of tracking down Sebastian Rossi and that Adrian West bitch, who needed to be eliminated.

"Yara," Fairuza said, approaching her cautiously, but Yara held up her hand, marching over to another one of the parked SUVs and yanking open the door.

She was furious with Fairuza for losing Sebastian; she'd berated her until Fairuza had broken down and wept, but her tears and blubbering apologies weren't enough. Fairuza needed a warning.

All of them did.

Karima sat inside, looking pale and terrified. Yara glared down at her. She'd done her duty as a D.O.C. member by contacting her, but she'd allowed West and the others to escape. She had to be punished.

"Get out," Yara ordered shortly.

Karima obeyed, stumbling out of the car and lowering her head in shame.

"I will ask you again. What were they looking for?" Yara demanded.

"I-I told you, they didn't tell me," Karima stammered. "All I know was it had something to do with Cleopatra. That's why I contacted you."

"They must have known something. They took some artifacts, did they not?"

"Yes, but those have already been indexed and catalogued. If there was anything of value, I would have told you!"

Her patience at its end, Yara took out her gun and pointed it at Karima, whose eyes widened with fear.

"Your duty was simple. If there was anything, *anything* of note at that museum, you were to notify me immediately. You were clearly mistaken."

"But we found nothing of note! I don't know what they think they found!" Karima cried, her voice wavering with fear.

Using the butt of her weapon, Yara hit Karima

across the face. Karima let out a cry and stumbled to her knees.

Yara closed her eyes, fury running through her veins. Karima had failed in her duty. There *must* be something among those artifacts, something that would lead to the treasure. That's why West had taken them.

Now the treasure was slipping from her grasp. And it was the fault of the weak, whimpering woman sprawled out on the ground before her.

Yara hardened her heart and murmured a prayer of apology to the goddess. Karima had failed her, and the Daughters.

Now she must pay.

She opened her eyes, leveled her weapon at Karima's head, and fired.

Karima crumpled to the ground, dead.

Yara turned to Leonid and Fairuza. They had opposite reactions to what she had just done. Leonid, she noted with annoyance and disgust, looked turned on, his eyes filled with lust, while Fairuza looked pale-faced with shock. She held Fairuza's gaze, wanting to communicate to her the cost of failure.

"Get rid of the body. And I want updates about West's possible location *yesterday*. They couldn't have gotten far. We can still catch up to them."

As Fairuza, Leonid and her men scrambled to obey her orders, Yara walked away, determination filling her, replacing her now ebbing fury.

She wouldn't let the treasure elude her.

Anyone who stood in the way would pay the price.

~

Cairo, Egypt
10:01 P.M.

ADRIAN TOOK in their surroundings as Julien pulled up to an upscale apartment building in Cairo's affluent Zamalek district. The apartment belonged to Julien's mother, who was currently out of the country on a dig in Southeast Asia. While Julien kept an apartment of his own in Cairo, they knew it wasn't wise to go there. His apartment was the first place the bureau—or Yara—would look.

Zamalek was located between Cairo and Giza, home to the famous pyramids, and had once been a stop for fisherman on Gezira Island in the Nile. It was now one of the more expensive districts in the city, a common dwelling place of the wealthy and expatriates alike who settled in Cairo. It was filled with modern residential streets dotted with cafés, restaurants, galleries, and traditional *ahwas*: Egyptian tea rooms.

After Julien parked in an adjoining garage, they headed inside the building. Despite Julien's insistence that it was empty, Adrian's old training kicked in and she and Nick checked every nook and cranny of the spacious apartment to ensure they were alone. It was definitely the apartment of an archaeologist, with models of artifacts from digs perched in various spots in the living room, and photographs of exotic dig locations from Thailand to India decorating the walls.

After they ate the sandwiches Julien brought them from the kitchen, they moved to a large table in the dining room, where they carefully spread out the artifacts they'd taken from the museum in El Qantara.

Adrian and Nick watched as both Julien and Sebastian looked over the items in careful detail.

"I'm not seeing anywhere a message could be hidden, or anything obvious. With the amethyst ring, there was an area beneath the stone to hide a message," Sebastian said after some time, with a heavy sigh. "That's not the case with these artifacts."

"It was always a long shot that we'd find anything among a handful of random artifacts," Julien said grimly.

"In her last moments," Adrian said, after a brief stretch of silence, "what would Cleopatra have been focused on? Obviously, the ring was engraved long beforehand, so we can assume she was prepared to send a secret message to her children."

"A message that only they would understand, something hidden from the Romans," Sebastian added, following her line of thinking. "That would have been tantamount."

"The Romans were well aware of Isis. Her cult was even worshipped in Rome," Julien added, leaning back in his chair. "So why hide a message to her children in one of the temples?"

"Romans for the most part didn't interfere in Egyptian religion," Sebastian said. "That was true for most of the regions they conquered. It's likely that the priests of Isis were loyal to her. They could have been a conduit for secret messages."

"How would Cleopatra expect a message from the temple of Isis in Egypt to get to her children? She must have known they'd be taken to Rome in a triumph," Julien said.

Adrian considered this. Roman triumphs were military processions undertaken by successful commanders after defeating an enemy, during which they would march through the streets of Rome with the spoils of their victory, including military captives, something that the proud Cleopatra would no doubt have wanted to avoid.

Cleopatra's children didn't avoid this fate, with Augustus marching them through the streets in a triumphal not long after his annexation of Egypt.

They continued to brainstorm but came up empty, soon deciding it was time to get some much-needed rest, though Adrian doubted she'd sleep. She knew she had to try; rest would clear the cobwebs from her fatigued brain.

But first, there was something she needed to do. She stopped Sebastian before he could head to one of the guest rooms Julien directed him to.

"Now that we're in Cairo, I think we should take you the embassy. I may have my differences with the feds right now, but you'll be safer with them."

"I knew you would say that," Sebastian said, giving her a knowing smile. "I've thought a lot about this since I escaped that madwoman. And . . . as long as my abductors are out there, I'm still in danger, which means so are Mira and Celeste. I have to see this through."

"Sebastian," Adrian said warily, shaking her head. First Julien, now Sebastian. "You barely escaped with your life this time. What if—"

"Cleopatra's treasure is something I've theorized for a long time, and it's coming to fruition. It's why Yara abducted me; she knows I'm crucial to finding this treasure. Let me help you find it before she does."

"I can't force you to go to the embassy," Adrian said after a long pause. "But I want you to promise me that if we face more danger, you'll go to the authorities. Mira will kick my ass if anything happens to you."

He offered her a light chuckle. "I've no doubt of that. You have my word."

Adrian hesitated, and he raised his eyebrows, sensing that she wanted to ask him something more.

"This may sound petty, but why did you never tell me your theory? About Cleopatra and this treasure?"

"It had nothing to do with not trusting you, if that's what you're worried about," Sebastian said quickly. "I've always thought it was a fringe theory and haven't shared it with anyone. There was simply no solid proof; it was only conjecture. Even when the artifacts were discovered, I thought it was far-fetched. But in the slight case that it wasn't, I wanted to share it with only a couple of people who were experts in the time period and Cleopatra— Roberta and Julien. I thought if there was any credence to my theory, the less people who knew about it, the better. I should have kept it to myself. After what happened to Roberta . . ." He trailed off, guilt flickering across his face.

"You can't blame yourself for what happened to her."

"Easier said than done," Sebastian said with a sigh. "I could never have envisioned any of this happening. Adrian," he continued, his voice wavering, "during my time with Yara . . . I've never seen someone so obsessed. She won't stop. She won't hesitate to eliminate anyone in her way."

"I know," Adrian said, recalling with a chill the ruthlessness in Yara's eyes when she'd raised her gun and fired at her. "You forget that I'm used to monsters like her. You let me handle Yara," Adrian said firmly.

Adrian gave Sebastian one last determined look before heading to her guest room, realizing how much she meant it.

Something was slowly coming back to life

within her after so many years out of law enforcement. A desire to stop people like Yara. It was as if she herself was coming back to life.

She wouldn't let Yara harm Sebastian, or the many others she intended to harm by carrying out her plans.

She wouldn't let her get near Cleopatra's treasure.

CHAPTER 28

Cairo, Egypt
12:15 A.M.

Sebastian sat at the dining room table, using a special digital microscope Julien had on hand to carefully look over each artifact for what felt like the millionth time.

The others had retired to their guest bedrooms, but Sebastian knew he wouldn't be able to sleep. His discussion with Adrian earlier that evening still weighed heavily on his mind.

Sighing with frustration, he set down the microscope and glanced at the time. He knew what would make him feel better. Another call with Mira.

He'd spoken with her briefly during the drive to Cairo, but he wanted a longer conversation with his wife.

Using a cell phone Julien had lent him, Sebastian dialed his wife's number.

"Sweetheart," Mira said, picking up on the first ring, and a rush of emotion swept over him. It wasn't long ago that he'd feared never seeing her again, and hearing her voice now was like a panacea for his soul.

"I love you," he said in reply, his voice heavy with emotion. "You and Celeste. So much. Is she there?"

"She's sleeping. She tried to stay awake, but I made her sleep. I couldn't follow my own advice," Mira said. "Seb, when will we see you?"

Sebastian closed his eyes, forcing himself to hold on to his resolve. She had asked him the same thing during their earlier phone call, and he'd told her he needed to get to safety first. But now it was time to tell her what he'd decided to do.

"Seb—" Mira gasped, when he told her he was going to stay with Adrian to keep looking for the treasure.

"Think about Celeste," Sebastian interrupted.

He could practically feel his wife's hesitance, her wavering, on the other end of the line. He knew that bringing up Celeste was the only thing that would convince her. His selfless wife would have no concern for her own safety but would do anything for Celeste.

He and Mira had tried for years to conceive a child. Doctor after doctor had told them it would be near impossible due to fertility issues Mira suffered from. Given their advancing ages, they hadn't considered adoption as it could be a timely process, and just when they'd given up hope that they'd ever have a child of their own, Mira had gotten pregnant. Celeste was their miracle, and they'd do anything for her.

When Mira spoke again, her voice was heavy with emotion. "Be careful, Seb," she said. "And come back to us."

"I will," Sebastian said, ignoring the tug of fear that pulled at his heart. He had to see this through.

1:30 A.M.

Adrian couldn't sleep.

The bed in the guest bedroom was plush and comfortable. She was beyond exhausted, having barely slept since Nick's fateful call in Rome. Yet sleep eluded her.

She kept thinking about their lack of progress with the artifacts. What if they were missing something?

Something vital.

She soon heard the low murmur of voices outside of her bedroom and got up, tugging on her jeans before padding out to the dining room. There, she found Julien and Sebastian huddled over the artifacts in deep discussion. Nick hovered behind them, nursing a cup of tea.

"No one invited me to the party?" she asked,

giving them a rueful smile as she joined them at the table.

"I don't think any of us are going to be able to sleep with such an intriguing archeological mystery on our hands," Julien said.

"I'm assuming no progress?" Adrian asked, rubbing her eyes.

"No," Sebastian confessed. "I'm thinking that if there is or was a message, it's long gone. Or we're looking in the wrong place."

Adrian considered this, recalling something she'd learned at the FBI academy years ago when she was training to become a criminal profiler.

"Always," her instructor had told her and her classmates, "assume that you are most likely wrong about your first assumption."

"What if it's not Pelusium?" Adrian asked, looking at Sebastian. "What if we're looking in the wrong place? You said the inscription read—"

"The fourth port city," Sebastian said.

"There were four port cities in Cleopatra's day, right? What made you land on Pelusium?"

"I conjectured that her trajectory was from west to east, starting with Alexandria," Sebastian said slowly.

"What if that's the wrong direction? What if the message is pointing to Alexandria?" Adrian pressed.

"Because Alexandria was a dangerous place for her followers after her fall," Sebastian said with a frown. "It was under Roman control. I don't understand why she would send her children to a city that her enemy had just conquered."

"Because," Julien spoke up, meeting Adrian's eyes, "she still had supporters there. There must have been someone willing to get a message to her children."

Sebastian still didn't look convinced. "Alexandria was full of temples dedicated to the goddess Isis in Cleopatra's time. And the one we know she had built during her lifetime has been long lost."

"And where would we even begin to look?" Nick added.

"We have to think . . . where would Cleopatra send her children? I know you have your doubts, Sebastian, but if it is Alexandria, it would've had to be somewhere secure. Somewhere her children would have known to go," Adrian said.

There was a long stretch of silence as they considered her words. Sebastian was shaking his head, but the more Adrian thought about it, the more Alexandria made sense. It was the capital city of the Ptolemies, their royal seat, the location of their massive palace, their—

Adrian froze. She looked up at them, swallowing hard. "This is going to sound crazy," she said.

"We need every idea," Nick responded. "What are you thinking?"

"The most obvious place," Adrian said. "Cleopatra's palace."

CHAPTER 29

*S*ilence fell over the room at Adrian's words. Sebastian and Julien frowned, doubt infusing their expressions.

"Think about it. Her children grew up there, knew every nook and cranny. Even if it was in the hands of the Romans, they would have known to go there. And like you said, Julien, Cleopatra's supporters didn't just disappear after her fall. There must have been someone there to aid them."

They all seemed to consider her words, but Sebastian's expression remained doubtful. "I'll give your theory some credence," he said finally. "But Cleopatra's palace is now submerged underwater and most of its artifacts have been excavated."

Adrian paused. She knew that over a thousand years ago, a massive earthquake triggered a tsunami that slammed into Alexandria. Cleopatra's palace was submerged beneath the waters of the Mediterranean, where they lay until the French archaeologist Franck Goddio discovered the ruins in the 1990s.

"Most," Adrian said. "Not all, right?"

Sebastian gave her a grudging nod. "The ones that remain haven't been moved out of concern for their fragility."

They were interrupted by the sound of screeching tires on asphalt and the roar of multiple car engines.

Sebastian paled and Adrian shot to her feet, Nick on her heels. Careful to stay out of sight, she partially opened the curtains of the living room window and peered out.

Several black cars had pulled up to the front of Julien's building.

Someone had found them.

~

2:02 *AM*

BRIGGS STALKED toward Julien Caron's apartment building, irritation coursing through him. Despite his status as the lead agent in Rome's field office, he was trailing behind Special Agent Meghan Farino, the agent in charge at Cairo's FBI headquarters, and two junior agents.

They had sent a second team of agents to Julien Caron's apartment in central Cairo. Briggs had a hunch that Caron would come to his mother's apartment instead, likely thinking it was safer, so he'd chosen to come to this location.

Ever since he'd arrived at Cairo's FBI office, Farino and the other agents had treated him like he was a foreign invader even though they were all supposed to be on the same side. Farino, younger than him by at least twenty years, had been dismissive since the moment he'd arrived on-site, treating him as an underling rather than a seasoned colleague. Farino was an expert in counterterrorism and had helped foil a major attack on the US embassy in Tunisia, earning her the position she now held in Cairo's field office.

Briggs had assumed she would find the information he'd provided about the Daughters of Cleopatra more than useful, but she'd informed him that they didn't have any such group on their radar or any information on the names of Yara or Leonid. She seemed to think that Sebastian's abductors were merely after more artifacts and that this was a simple case of attempted art theft.

Briggs gritted his teeth. The counterterrorism outfit seemed to believe they were above art crimes as the agency's main goal was counterterrorism ever since 9/11. But what the Cairo office didn't seem to realize was that if what Sebastian had told him was true, this Yara and her cronies would unleash a series of terrorist attacks, using Cleopatra's treasure as their financial backing.

Farino was more invested in finding West and

bringing her in, though Briggs now doubted that they should be focused on her, given everything he'd learned from Sebastian.

Perhaps it would have been easy to focus on West for *just* Roberta Fields' murder, but her murder hadn't been an isolated incident. Everything that had happened simply didn't add up. There was the burglary back at Sebastian's apartment in New York, Sebastian's abduction, the encounter West had with the intruder at the American University of Rome, and her rescue of Sebastian from his abductors.

This was about more than just some stolen artifacts. Sebastian telling him that his abductors were after a massive treasure made the most sense for someone to go to such lengths—including murder—to obtain it.

Determination overtook his anger, and he forced his way past Farino and the agents in front of him, holding up his hand when Farino started to knock. She glared at him, but he ignored her. At the very least, he would be the one to approach West and his rogue agent. He wanted to let them know he no longer considered West a suspect, but he needed them to tell him everything they'd learned since fleeing Rome to help him apprehend Sebastian's abductors; the people who'd likely murdered Roberta Fields and the young security guard.

As he lifted his hand to knock, the door swung open.

Stunned, he took in the person who'd opened the door. It wasn't Julien Caron, nor West or Agent Harper.

It was Sebastian Rossi.

"Agent Briggs," he said calmly. "I've been expecting you."

SEBASTIAN'S PULSE raced with anxiety as he sat across from Briggs, Farino, and two other stern-looking FBI agents.

When Adrian and Nick had recognized Agent Briggs, they'd acted quickly.

It was Adrian's idea to have Sebastian stay behind. He'd initially refused, wanting to stay with the others, but Adrian had been insistent. They needed him to buy time for them to escape; Julien had enough expertise to help them with any potential finds they'd make with Cleopatra's submerged palace. As determined as he'd been to stick with them—he was serious about wanting to see this through—he'd grudgingly relented. He had to admit that a small part of him was relieved; he was eager to see his wife and daughter again.

Now, he would just have to trust that Adrian and the others would beat Yara to the treasure.

He leaned forward, focusing on Agent Briggs. "Before I say anything, I want assurances that my wife and daughter will be protected. The woman who kept me prisoner had them under surveillance and continually threatened their lives."

"Of course," Briggs said immediately. "I already have an agent on your wife and daughter."

Relief settled over Sebastian, though he knew he wouldn't fully relax until he was physically with his family.

As if reading his mind, Briggs held his gaze. "I'll be happy to bring you to Mira and Celeste. And I wanted to—"

The woman, Farino, interrupted him. "We'll want to question you further about your abduction, but you can help us first with one important question. Where is Adrian West and Agent Harper?"

Briggs' mouth tightened, but he remained silent. Sebastian took a breath; he was prepared for this question. He hoped he could maintain his poker face.

"I don't know where they went. They didn't want to tell me for my own protection. Again, they're not the ones you should be looking for. I gave you the names of the people who abducted me. Adrian and Agent Harper rescued me."

"Until we can confirm what you've told us, West remains a person of interest. All we need to do is talk to her and we can get this all straightened out," Farino said, giving him a tight smile.

Sebastian studied the young woman. For a federal agent, she was a terrible liar. Despite what he'd told them about his abductors, she still seemed razor focused on Adrian. His gaze shifted to Briggs, who remained silent, his expression neutral.

"I told you I don't know where Adrian went," Sebastian lied. "But I'm happy to answer any questions you have about my abduction or my captors. And then I want to see my wife and daughter."

.

CHAPTER 30

Alexandria, Egypt
5:02 A.M.

*A*drian took in the expanse of the city as Julien drove through the streets of Alexandria.

Today's Alexandria was a bustling coastal city filled with modern buildings that housed both apartments and businesses, dotted with monuments that signaled to its grand historical past.

Now, in the early morning, it was quiet, a hint of salt in the air from the breeze coming in off the Mediterranean. But as the city awoke, its streets would teem with cars, tourists, and locals alike. Amid the sounds of honking horns and vendors hawking their wares, the sound of the call to prayer would beckon the faithful.

In Cleopatra's day, Alexandria had been a cosmopolitan city, akin to a Paris or Milan of the modern age, home to a multicultural population, impressive Hellenic academic institutions and stunning monuments that fused both Hellenic and Egyptian religions and traditions. Even now, she could almost taste the ancient spices that once scented the air and hear the multitude of old tongues from Greek to Latin to Egyptian. It was no surprise that the Ptolemies had ruled from nowhere else but Alexandria during their centuries of ruling over Egypt.

Julien drove along the busy El Gaish Road toward the Citadel of Qaitbay, an old medieval fortress built along the city's harbor. It was near here that the boat that would take them on their dive awaited them.

She was glad that they'd left Sebastian with the feds, though she knew how much he'd wanted to stick with them. Despite her lingering differences with her former employer—including the fact that they thought she was a murderer—she knew he was safer with them.

She hoped their trip to Cleopatra's submerged palace brought forth new information. They had come here not only to evade the feds but to look at the ruins of the palace in person. Julien had pulled up some digital footage of the ruins he had access to on his iPad, but they had revealed nothing telling, and they were limited. Some images were difficult or impossible to make out, as there were many arti-facts that hadn't been moved since antiquity due to their fragile state. Their best bet was to look at the ruins in person in the hope that they'd discover something significant.

If there was no clue to be found at the submerged palace, they were back to where they started. Or worse yet, Yara and her cronies would have a leg up on them.

"I can practically hear your thoughts," Nick observed.

"I'm just hoping this isn't a wasted trip," she said, meeting Nick's concerned gaze.

"Agreed," Nick said. "But you were right back there. This is worth looking into. And as for Yara, now that she doesn't have Sebastian— someone she clearly needs—we can assume she's desperate now and left in the dark."

Adrian nodded, hoping that he was right.

They soon reached the harbor that hugged Alexandria's coastline. Julien parked and turned to them. "Remember our cover story, and let me do most of the talking," he said.

"You're the boss," Nick said, holding up his hands.

Julien had contacted Hekmat Ayad, the owner of a local tour company whom both he and Sebastian were friendly with, giving him the cover story that he and two colleagues needed to look at Cleopatra's underwater palace for a joint presentation they were going to give: a similar lie he'd told Kamara in El Qantara.

Hekmat was a stout Egyptian man who gave them wary but polite looks as they approached him on the dock. By the look on his face, Adrian doubted he bought Julien's story about why they needed to look at Cleopatra's underwater palace so last minute, but the thousand euros Julien had offered him must have quelled any misgivings.

"Hekmat," Julien said, greeting him with a wide smile. "Thank you for doing this."

"Anything I can do for an old friend," Hekmat said, giving them both nods as Julien introduced Adrian and Nick, before helping them onto the dive boat, the aptly named *Cleopatra's Treasure*.

Hekmat guided the boat out to the center of the bay, whose blue waters glittered beneath the rising sun. When he stopped the boat, he stepped away from the prow to prep Julien and Adrian for their dive.

Nick was going to stay above as a lookout while she and Julien dove, as he wasn't a certified diver. She knew it was also partially because of Nick's deep-seated fear of drowning after an incident in the Bahamas in his teens.

Adrian was a relatively strong swimmer and had gone scuba diving several times in her life, though it hadn't been for some time since her last trip . . . and there certainly hadn't been as much at stake.

After Hekmat reviewed the safety protocols with them, she and Julien went to private rooms inside the boat's cabin and changed into their scuba diving gear, consisting of a wetsuit, diving mask, scuba gloves, and fins. Hekmat helped them both with their tanks, submersible pressure gauges, regulators, compasses, and dive computers. He also gave them underwater torches and backup dive lights.

Finally, they were ready. She turned to Nick, who gave her a reassuring nod, before diving after Julien into the waters, praying that some revelation would be revealed in the depths.

~

Port Said, Egypt
5:15 A.M.

YARA BOARDED the small private plane, her pulse thrumming with anticipation. She took a seat and buckled herself in, clenching her fists in her lap, willing herself to calm her breathing.

She had decamped to the airport at Port Said with Leonid, Fairuza and Markos, who had arrived from Rome several hours ago with a bandaged leg. Though she could tell his injury caused him some lingering pain, he insisted he was fine.

She'd noticed Leonid looking at her with jealousy when she spoke to his brother and made a show of standing closer to Markos and touching his arm. Perhaps a little sexual rivalry would increase Leonid's devotion to her and make him screw up less.

Yara was determined to leave at a moment's notice once she received even a hint of West's whereabouts. She hadn't slept a wink, periodically getting out of the plane to pace and stretch her legs, willing the frustration to seep from her veins.

Now, after a tense and restless night, she could finally smile. She had just learned of the where-abouts of Adrian West and her allies. She had a night guard, Zosar, on the Daughters' payroll who patrolled the dock that led to Cleopatra's under-water palace, keeping track of anyone who visited the docks outside of the regular tour hours. Ever since losing the professor, she had reached out to all of her contacts with descriptions of West, Harper, Caron and Sebastian Rossi, informing them all on pain of death to alert her if they were spotted.

She had received the call from Zosar, who was just ending his shift when he recognized Adrian and her colleagues from her description. This had immediately lightened her mood, as her FBI contact had informed her that Sebastian was in their custody. Even with her contact in place, it would be too risky to retrieve him from their hands.

She knew then that her best bet was West herself leading her to the treasure.

The news that West had arrived at the docks was a like a gift from the goddess herself. The plane could get them to Alexandria in an hour. From experience, she knew such a dive, including prep time, could take hours, but she wanted to ensure that she didn't lose them, and had given Zosar an incentive with the promise of a handsome financial reward to keep them there.

After the plane had taken off and reached

cruising altitude, Fairuza approached Yara with her head bowed. Fairuza had been avoiding Yara ever since she'd killed Karima; even now she approached her like she was a barely tethered wild animal.

"What?" Yara snapped.

"I-I wanted to apologize again. For—for my failure," Fairuza said, her eyes filling with tears. She sank to her knees before Yara. "Daughters has changed my life. It means everything to me. The last thing I ever want to do is to fail you, or it. Please forgive me."

Yara studied Fairuza, wondering if she was speaking out of fear or genuine remorse. She told herself it didn't matter; the outcome would be the same. Fairuza wouldn't fail her again.

She took Fairuza's chin in her hand, tilting her head up so that she was looking at her.

"I forgive you," she said. "But I will give you no more chances. I've been quite merciful. Do not fail me again."

MEDITERRANEAN SEA
    5:20 *A.M.*

Adrian had forgotten how peaceful she found the underwater depths, the silence and tranquility of life beneath the waves. Though the water was murky, with the help of her underwater torch she could make out several schools of fish pass by as she and Julien dove farther down.

Under different circumstances, this would have been a relaxing dive. But now, her senses were razor focused as she scanned the floor of the bay as she descended.

Julien had told her he'd made this dive several times before. He was familiar with where to go. She trailed Julien as he dove to the seabed, swimming forward until they reached the first of the group of ruins.

Awe consumed her as she took them in. As much as she'd learned about Cleopatra and the magnificent palace she'd once lived in, and even having seen the photos herself, there was *nothing* like seeing them in person.

She could see ancient red granite columns resting on the sea floor like sleeping giants. There were the fragments of a large bowl, an old amphora, the ruins of several statues, a stone with a carved design she didn't recognize. There was even stone from the great lighthouse that had once stood just outside of Alexandria, one of the ancient wonders of the world.

One of the most distinctive ruins was that of a headless sphinx embedded into the ground, the design of it impressive even as a ruin; she could clearly make out the indentation of the thigh's curve.

Julien made a hand signal pointing forward, drawing her attention away from the sphinx. She followed his gaze to a statue of the goddess Isis that was partially embedded in the sand.

They swam forward, taking it in. It was on its side and appeared even more delicate than the headless sphinx; she could see why it had been left beneath the waters.

Julien was studying it closely, running his underwater torch over it. He stilled as he shined the light on its base.

Adrian followed his gaze, and her heart plummeted in her chest at what she saw.

CHAPTER 31

Mediterranean Sea
5:40 A.M.

drian stared at the base of the statue, adrenaline coursing through her veins.

Jutting out beneath the sandy sea floor, there was the barest trace of an inscription at its base. She could only make out a curved line. Julien swam forward and gingerly brushed away the sand, revealing the rest of the inscription.

Adrian swam forward, using her underwater torch to illuminate the faint inscription, now whittled away to barely a trace. Though it was faint, she could make out the same inscription that Sebastian told her was on the amethyst ring—the sun and moon. The symbols for Cleopatra's twins, Cleopatra Selene and Alexander Helios.

Yet there was more to the inscription.

Beneath the faint traces of the sun and moon

were three hieroglyphs. Adrian could only make out the impression of an eye, not able to discern the other two. Julien swam even closer and snapped several photos with his underwater camera as Adrian held up her torch to provide him with as much illumination as possible.

As she took in the faint inscription, a surge of emotion swelled in her chest. There was no doubt in her mind that this was another message from Cleopatra to her children, buried for centuries beneath the waters of the Mediterranean. The hieroglyphs had to be significant. They had to do whatever they could to make them out.

Once Julien had taken multiple photos of the inscription, they both resurfaced, with Hekmat and Nick helping them back onto the boat and divesting them of their gear.

"We found something," Adrian said as soon as she caught her breath, giving Nick a wide grin.

Julien took out his camera, turning it around so she and Nick could look at the photos he'd taken of the inscription.

"Wow," Nick breathed, taking in the faint traces of the sun and moon. "How has no one noticed this before?"

"I've seen footage of the ruins many times and I've seen it live on dives, yet even I missed it. The markings are so faded, they're hard to make out, and even if you could, without the context that we're looking for, it looks no different from inscriptions honoring other gods on other statues. Unless you're looking for it, it would be next to impossible to tell that this is a secret message."

"Can you tell what the hieroglyphs say?" Nick pressed.

"They're very difficult to make out," Julien said, frowning. "There's definitely a hieroglyph of an eye, which can mean several things—to make, to see, to be watchful . . ."

"It can even mean blindness," Adrian added. "We need to know what the other two hieroglyphs mean to make sense of it."

"Thus far, the codes have led to places. Could these hieroglyphs refer to a place?" Nick asked.

"I don't know what place an eye could refer to," Julien said.

"I think it's something more specific," Adrian murmured. She stared at the symbol of the eye, thinking of all its various meanings. *To see, to make, to watch.*

She studied the other two hieroglyphs, trying to figure out how they could connect to the eye but came up empty.

"As the non-linguist slash historian in the group, I'm going to be the layperson here," Nick said finally. "That rectangular thing beneath the eye? It looks kind of like a chair."

Adrian took the camera from Julien, zooming in on the image. It did indeed look like a chair.

Her heart leapt into her throat. She couldn't believe she hadn't seen it before. Julien met her gaze, a grin spreading across his face, seeming to come to the same conclusion she had.

"Want to let me in on this look you two are sharing? Do you think I'm crazy or—" Nick began.

"Nick," Adrian said, beaming. "You are a genius."

Nick looked baffled. Adrian pointed at the rectangular shape. "That *is* a hieroglyph of a chair. Well, a sort of chair. It's a throne."

"OK . . . " Nick said slowly. "Again, layperson here. You're going to have to explain. So . . . the hieroglyph is referring to some sort of king?"

"Slightly above a king," Julien said. He pointed to the inscription on the camera, zooming in as tightly as possible and holding it up for them to see. "If this hieroglyph is an eye, and the hieroglyph beneath it is a throne, that can only mean that this other glyph is that of a seated god."

"Which means the hieroglyph literally spells out W-S-I-R. But we're most familiar with the Latinized term from ancient Greek, which is itself from ancient Egyptian. It spells out Osiris," Adrian said.

Nick looked awestruck, taking in the inscription. "OK, there's a hieroglyph for Osiris beneath Cleopatra's terms for her children. What could it mean?"

"That's the ultimate question," Adrian said with a sigh. Her giddiness over realizing the hieroglyphs referred to Osiris was rapidly fading. Where could it be pointing to?

"If it's a temple dedicated to Osiris, we're screwed," Julien said bluntly. "There were temples dedicated to Osiris all over Egypt, many of which are lost to time."

"We thought the same thing about temples dedicated to Isis," Nick pointed out. "And look what we just found."

"Yes, but this was literally at Cleopatra's palace, and the ring pointed us here. We don't have anything else other than the hieroglyph referring to Osiris," Adrian said, a renewed frustration surging through her.

The sudden motor of a boat approaching pulled their attention away from the camera. Hekmat, who'd been hovering on the opposite end of the boat, pretending not to listen to their conversation as he packed their gear away, looked up with a frown.

Adrian tensed as the man on the boat, who looked official with a security guard's uniform, stopped his boat close to theirs. He spoke to Hekmat in rapid Arabic; he seemed unnecessarily hostile.

Unease settled over her gut, and she exchanged a look with Nick, who also tensed.

"What's going on?" Nick asked in a low voice.

"The guard—Hekmat is calling him Zosar—is claiming he didn't submit the proper paperwork or pay the fees for this dive," Adrian said, frowning.

Julien stepped forward to intervene, but instinct had Adrian reach for his arm, keeping him back. Something about this whole interaction seemed off.

It turned out her instincts were correct.

She watched in horror as the security guard calmly took out a gun and pointed it at Hekmat, shooting him point-blank in the chest. Hekmat hit the deck with a thud.

He turned to Adrian, Nick and Julien, his tone ice cold as he said, in heavily accented English, "Get into the cabin below deck, or someone else dies."

CHAPTER 32

Mediterranean Sea
7:02 *A.M.*

*A*drian kept her gaze steadily trained on their captor, Zosar, though panic, anger and guilt still flowed through her veins. Hekmat had been caught in the crossfire and was dead because he'd helped them.

She was in the cabin below deck, on her knees, with her hands behind her head, along with Nick and Julien. At her side, Nick's body was taut with tension, while Julien trembled with fear.

Adrian forced herself to set aside her tumultuous feelings and kept her focus on Zosar. She could assume that he worked for Yara and the Daughters, which chilled her to the bone. How far was Yara's reach? Unlike Kamara, he was eerily calm, his eyes cold. She'd seen that look before, in the eyes of those who'd killed before and wouldn't hesitate to kill again.

Professional down to the bone; there was no feeling in his eyes though he'd just committed cold-blooded murder. Perhaps he was a mercenary as an extra job in addition to working as security. He reminded her of Leonid with that air of cold and determined professionalism.

Mercenary, she thought slowly, an idea suddenly striking her. He was holding them here for a reason; she suspected it was until Yara arrived.

"How much is she paying you?" Adrian asked him in Arabic.

Zosar stiffened slightly but remained tight-lipped. She could feel the gazes of Nick and Julien on her, but she kept her gaze trained on the man. *Trust me,* she pleaded to them silently.

"My friend can double whatever she's paying you," Adrian continued, hoping that Julien would go along with her hastily put-together plan.

"Shut up," Zosar hissed, but she could see the flare of greed in his dark eyes.

"Julien, how much do you think you could wire to his account?" she asked, never taking her eyes off Zosar.

"Ten thousand euros for the first transaction, fifty for the second," he said. Though his voice wavered a bit, she was surprised by how steadfast he sounded. How confident.

Zosar's hand wavered on his gun; she could see the hunger in his eyes. Adrian continued, hoping to keep him intrigued, "I know about Yara and her organization. I know she's not loyal to those who work for her. What do you think she'll do to you once she's gotten what she wants? She won't leave witnesses. She has no loyalty to you."

Again, that flicker in his eyes. She could see that she was getting to him. Slowly.

"Help us instead," she implored. "All you have to do is let us go and you'll be sixty thousand euros richer."

There was a tense, long pause that stretched. Zosar held her gaze as if searching for any hint of deception. She willed her expression to remain neutral, not letting her gaze waver.

"One hundred thousand," he said, and Adrian's heart leapt, but she kept her expression neutral.

"One hundred thousand. Can you do that, Julien?"

"I can have it wired to whatever account you want in an hour," Julien said.

"But first you have to get us off of this boat," Adrian said. "The longer we wait, the more likely it is that Yara will get here and eliminate all of us, and we won't be able to make our deal."

"I will need a deposit first," Zosar said, scowling.

"We can do that," Julien said.

After several more tense seconds, Zosar took a step back, keeping the gun trained on them.

"Stand up—slowly," he warned, this time in English for Nick's benefit.

221

Though Nick's Arabic was halting at best, she could tell by his tight, coiled expression that he knew the gist of what was going on.

And that he was ready.

Adrian, Nick and Julien stood. Zosar took another step back toward the steps leading out of the cabin, but before he could bark out another order, Adrian and Nick moved in tandem.

Adrian darted forward, kicking at Zosar's legs, and Nick tackled him to the ground, pinning him with all of his body weight while Adrian disarmed him. Nick punched Zosar several times, lifting his head up and smashing it down on the deck, rendering him unconscious.

She turned to Julien, who looked ashen.

"You OK?"

"Yeah," Julien said weakly.

"Good job playing along," she said, before her face turned serious. "Can you drive this thing? We need to get the hell out of here."

Julien nodded, and together they made their way to the deck. Julien paled even further at the sight of Hekmat's still body lying on the deck but made his way to the prow of the boat.

As Nick moved to cover Hekmat's body with a tarp that was lying on the deck, Adrian abruptly stilled when she heard the approaching motor of a boat.

"Get down!" she shouted as gunshots rained down onto the deck around them.

CHAPTER 33

Mediterranean Sea
7:15 A.M.

*A*drian, Nick and Julien hit the deck.

Adrian and Nick crouched low and moved toward the rear of the boat, returning fire.

"Julien!" she cried. "We need to go—now! We'll cover you!"

She and Nick kept their weapons trained on the approaching boat, firing, as Julien brought the boat's engine to a roar and sped off.

But the other boat kept on them, gaining distance fast. As it got closer, she could make out the figures of Yara, Leonid and two other men; they were the ones who were firing.

Soon, they would be on them.

Adrian and Nick ducked as the men kept up their fire, returning their own fire when they could.

But Adrian knew they couldn't hold them off for long.

Keeping low, Adrian peered over the edge of the deck, focusing on the driver of the boat. She crept along the deck, dodging bullets, making her way to the very rear of the boat.

"Adrian, what the hell are you doing?!" Nick shouted.

"Trust me!" she cried. She ignored the surrounding chaos, the cacophony of her heartbeat, and honed all her focus on the driver. She remained low to the deck as the other boat got closer . . . closer still . . .

And then she took her shot. Aiming her weapon, she trained it on the driver of the boat, firing off several shots.

The driver of the boat slumped over, immediately causing it to veer off course, buying them precious time.

"Julien—go!" she cried.

Julien sped up the boat, and it raced away, getting closer and closer to the docks. She had bought them some precious seconds, but it wouldn't be long before Yara's boat was once again on them.

She made her way back to Nick, who gave her both an impressed and scolding look; she returned it with a grin before readying her weapon and returning her focus to Yara's boat that was thankfully getting smaller in the distance.

"Julien!" she shouted over the roar of the boat's motor. "As soon as we get back to the docks, run!"

"You don't have to tell me twice!" Julien returned.

They made it to the docks moments later, with Yara's boat racing toward them in the distance.

As soon as they arrived, they leapt off the boat and dashed toward the parking lot, with Julien leaving the motor running—time was precious.

They stopped at the first car they reached as soon as they hit the parking lot, an old Volkswagen that screeched to a halt when Nick leveled his weapon at the stunned driver.

Wide-eyed and terrified, the driver stumbled out of the car, his hands up, as Adrian, Nick and Julien scrambled inside, with Julien taking the wheel, pressing the gas and speeding out of the parking lot and away from the docks.

～

Embassy of the United States - FBI Offices
Cairo, Egypt
8:02 A.M.

SEBASTIAN EMBRACED MIRA, holding her close as she wept into his arms. Celeste hovered next to them, her brown eyes shimmering with tears of her own.

He'd been at the FBI's headquarters in Cairo

for at least two hours as Farino and Briggs grilled him about Adrian and Nick's whereabouts and their activities during his time with them.

He'd told them all he could, except for where they were going next. Briggs didn't seem satisfied, seeming to sense that he was withholding information.

Finally, Sebastian had refused to say anything more. He wanted to see his wife and daughter, who had just arrived at a hotel close to the embassy.

Mira pulled back, wiping her tears away and giving him a rueful smile.

"Maybe you take a break from the academic conferences for a while," she said. He chuckled, touching his wife's face. He loved her so much; it terrified him how close he'd come to never seeing her again.

"Yeah, Dad," Celeste said, stepping forward as he embraced her. "Maybe try not getting kidnapped again."

Her voice was light, but he could detect her undercurrent of fear. He pressed a kiss to the top of his daughter's head.

"I'll try not to, kiddo," he said.

There was a sharp knock on the door of the conference room they were in. Briggs entered, his gaze hard as he focused on Sebastian.

"There's been a shooting at the Alexandria harbor," he said grimly. "From eyewitness accounts, it sounds like your former student and my rogue agent were involved. If there is anything you know, Professor, now is the time to be honest with me."

CHAPTER 34

Alexandria, Egypt
12:07 P.M.

drian paced the small motel room. A throbbing headache had formed at the base of her temple; she wryly wondered if too much thinking and continually hitting a brick wall caused it.

They had remained in Alexandria, with Julien taking various winding side streets to get deeper into the city. This had been her idea; Julien and Nick had wanted to put as much distance between them and Alexandria as possible. She had reasoned that Yara would assume they'd leave the city and have her men patrolling the roads leading out.

They'd come to the Karmouz neighborhood, an older part of Alexandria located in the southern part of the city. Needing to stay as off the grid as possible, they'd checked into a run-down motel that was far from the glittering tourist hotels along the harbor. Julien had checked in alone under a fake name while Nick and Adrian, her head covered in a scarf she'd found in their getaway car, entered through a back entrance.

Now they were eating a local staple of *eish fino*, a type of bread, and dates that Julien had procured for them from a local street vendor, trying to make sense of what they'd discovered and trying to determine where to go next.

So far they'd come up empty. The pressure was growing; Adrian knew they didn't have time to spare. It wasn't safe for them to stay in the same place for too long, given that both Yara and the FBI were on their tail.

"Using the same logic that led us to her palace should lead us to where the Osiris inscription points," Adrian said. "Perhaps somewhere else in Alexandria?"

"The palace is one of the few places we can get to in the modern area from her time, even if it is seriously eroded. The Ptolemaic-era Alexandria is long gone," Julien said, shaking his head.

"And why send her children to her palace just to send them somewhere else in Alexandria?" Nick asked. "Let's assume that the palace was relatively safe if people loyal to her were still working there. Alexandria was still under Roman control after her fall. It would have had to be somewhere safer for them to go to, right?"

"OK. Let's say this inscription leads to somewhere safer for Cleopatra's children. Somewhere outside of Alexandria. Julien, what do we know about Osiris? We know about Isis' significance to Cleopatra . . . what could Osiris' significance be?"

"Well, there's his famous myth. Seth was Osiris' jealous brother, who murdered him and tore his body into pieces, leaving them all over Egypt. Isis found the pieces and buried them, except for the phallus—hence Osiris' connection to rebirth, resurrection, fertility," Julien said. "Osiris was the god of rebirth and resurrection, but also of the dead and the underworld. In ancient Egypt, when the pharaoh died, he became Osiris, while the pharaoh's son would become the embodiment of Horus, his son."

Adrian considered his words. The notion of renewal and rebirth would be significant to a recently dethroned and defeated queen.

"What sites in Egypt are connected to Osiris?"

"Many. Religious festivals playing out the Osiris myth were performed all over Egypt. And there were temples all over Egypt dedicated to him," Julien said.

"Well, which sites still exist? Sites we could go to now?" Nick asked.

"There's the Osiris temple in Abydos, which is one of the most significant and oldest sites in Egypt," Julien said. "And there's also—"

He stopped himself, closing his eyes. Adrian frowned.

"Julien?" she pressed.

"I can't believe I didn't think of this before," Julien said with a heavy sigh. "There's the temple of Philae. The cults of both Isis and Osiris continued there long after Cleopatra's fall, into the fifth century CE. That temple was important to the Ptolemies; Cleopatra's father did renovations on it. It was sacred to the Egyptians; Philae was believed to be one of Osiris' resting places. And that's not all. The temple of Philae is in Upper Egypt, a place ripe for rebellion against invaders—including the Romans—and where many who were still loyal to Cleopatra lived."

A combination of excitement and hope flared to life within her at his words.

Adrian was familiar with the temple of Philae; it was one of the stops she'd made during the child-hood journey to Egypt with her parents. The temple of Philae would have been a relatively safe and sacred place for Cleopatra to send her children.

"Well," she said, grinning at Nick and Julien. "We know where we're going next."

CHAPTER 35

Alexandria Harbor
12:15 P.M.

Sebastian trailed Briggs as he made his way along Alexandria's harbor. Crime scene tape had been looped off around one of the anchored boats, and curious onlookers, from tourists to locals alike, had gathered to take in the scene.

Sebastian stared at Briggs' back, hoping he was right to put his trust in the man.

Back in the conference room at the embassy, Briggs had asked to speak to him alone when Sebastian still hesitated to tell him everything he knew. Mira and Celeste had left, reluctantly, but not before Mira gave Briggs one of her steely-eyed stares that she only gave Sebastian during one of their rare arguments.

"I know you don't trust me, and I understand why," Briggs said. "But you should know I no longer consider Adrian West a suspect."

At Sebastian's look of surprise, he continued, "My focus is now on this Daughters organization and the woman behind your abduction. It's my colleagues who are still focused on West; they're more concerned about the optics, given that Agent Harper is with her and she's a former agent. I just want to get to the bottom of all this, and I believe I can work with West and Agent Harper to do so. So even if you don't trust my colleagues, I need you to trust me."

Sebastian had studied Briggs' expression and saw nothing but sincerity there. He went with his instincts, and told Briggs everything he'd previously withheld.

Now, Briggs turned to look at Sebastian, gesturing for him to trail him aboard the boat that was now a crime scene. This was the boat Adrian, Nick and Julien had taken to dive among the ruins of Cleopatra's palace.

He faltered at the sight of dried blood on the deck. Briggs told him a body had been found on deck and identified him as Hekmat Ayad, a friend of Sebastian's. He'd gone on and directed many of his students to Hekmat's tours. Grief and anger filled him. Hekmat was a good man and didn't deserve such an end.

He swallowed back his emotions as a crime scene technician approached them, telling Briggs about the bullet casings they'd found and handing him a digital camera left behind by Adrian and the others.

"From what we can tell, it looks like dive pictures from the submerged palace," the tech said.

Briggs took the camera, frowning, before glancing over at Sebastian.

"Any idea of what they were looking for?"

Briggs handed him the camera, and Sebastian took it, flipping through the various images. He'd taken the dive to Cleopatra's palace several times—he'd learned how to dive just for the experience—and tried to figure out what they'd found. Sebastian took in the familiar photos, stumped . . . when he froze.

Several photos focused on something he'd never noticed before. It was very faint, comprising a hieroglyph of Osiris, along with an image of a moon and sun. The same moon and sun inscribed on the amethyst ring. *Cleopatra's twins.*

"Sebastian?" Briggs pressed.

Sebastian ignored him, closing his eyes as he tried to figure out what this meant. He mentally went through all he knew of Osiris, his temples, and where this message could lead.

There were several possibilities, but he focused on the one linked the closest to the Ptolemies.

"Sebastian?" Briggs asked again.

Sebastian's eyes flew open as it hit him. He took a shuddering breath.

"I think I know where they're going next."

∾

Airspace over Asyut, Egypt
3:37 *P.M.*

ADRIAN SAT NEXT to Nick and Julien in the rear of Julien's private plane, flipping through photos of the Philae temple on Julien's iPad.

Julien had contacted his pilot, who'd met them at Borg El Arab Airport just south of Alexandria. They'd abandoned their stolen car and taken a taxi from their small hotel, with Julien ordering the taxi driver with a generous tip to take side roads.

Now, they were on their way to Aswan International Airport in southern Egypt—Upper Egypt in Cleopatra's day—which was the closest airport to the Philae temple.

She studied the images of Philae as Julien told them more information about the temple complex. "The current island the complex is on, Agilkia Island, is not its original location. It was originally located near the First Cataract of the Nile."

"Why was it moved?" Nick asked.

"The great Nile. It kept getting flooded by the waters, so UNESCO undertook a massive, decades-long project in which they painstakingly deconstructed the temple, moved it to Agilkia Island, which is on higher ground to protect it from flooding. There, it was reconstructed."

"Wow," Nick said, letting out a whistle beneath his breath.

"You mentioned before that the Ptolemies reno-vated much of the buildings that make up the complex now?" Adrian asked.

"Yes, but there are buildings as ancient as from the time of the pharaoh Nectanebo I, who was the last native ruler of Egypt," Julien replied. "In Cleopatra's day, and even long before that, the complex was a site of pilgrimage for worshippers of Isis, for Egyptians and even Greeks. Even after Christianity was introduced to Egypt, the cult of Isis still flourished there due to continued worship by the local Nubians."

Adrian considered his words, continuing to take in images of the temple complex. She could imagine Cleopatra having devoted followers who would visit the temple. Perhaps priests as well? Someone to guard something hidden for her children?

The only thing she was grappling with was the fact that the temple complex had been thoroughly excavated. If there was a treasure there, someone would have found it, or it was long gone. If that were the case, she could only pray there was some other clue that led to a nearby destination, other-wise they were once again at a dead end.

Her thoughts remained focused on this possi-bility even as they landed and made their way to the dark SUV Julien had arranged for them. He'd foregone a driver, wanting to keep their destination as under wraps as possible.

As Julien drove out of the airport and onto the

road leading into Aswan, Adrian barely looked up from Julien's iPad, studying the layout of the temple, trying to determine what the best parts of the temple complex to examine were, when the SUV lurched forward—hard—as something barreled into them from behind.

Her head slammed onto the seat in front of her, and she let out a cry of pain, looking out of the windows in shock.

Several other SUVs pulled up to their vehicle with screeching tires, surrounding and boxing them in. Men armed with military-style rifles and dark uniforms got out, circling their vehicle, pointing their rifles right at them.

Icy fear coursed through Adrian's veins as she watched the familiar figure of a woman climb out of one of the SUVs, approaching them.

It was Yara.

And they were trapped.

CHAPTER 36

Aswan-Abu Simbel Road
Aswan, Egypt
5:12 P.M.

Adrian fought against the arms of the large, bear-like man who pulled her out of the SUV, forcing her roughly to her knees. The other soldiers did the same to both Nick and Julien, forcing them to their knees and placing their rifles against their backs.

She took in the men who surrounded them. They looked like soldiers, yet none of them wore the desert camouflage style of uniform that the Egyptian military wore. *Mercenaries*, she realized in a daze, as the man who'd dragged her out jabbed his rifle into her back.

Yara stepped forward, keeping her gaze trained on Adrian as she approached Nick, taking out a pistol and pressing it to his temple.

"Your choice is very simple, Adrian," she said calmly. "You tell me where you're going and what you've discovered, or I kill your boyfriend, Julien, and then you."

As YARA WATCHED the multitude of emotions filter over Adrian's face, from anguish to panic to terror, pleasure flowed through her veins. By the way Adrian was looking at Nick Harper, she had found the bitch's weakness.

Yes, Adrian clearly cared for Doctor Rossi, but there was no doubt she cared for the man with the pistol pressed to his head in a different way. *Foolish woman*, she thought. To put such emotional weight on a man. Yara had done that once before, and she'd barely escaped with her life. Men were tools to be used and nothing more.

It was hard to believe that hours earlier she'd been at a dead end. Adrian and her allies had escaped her—again—and she had no idea where to begin looking. Zosar had been useless, pleading for his life before Yara watched dispassionately as Leonid executed him. She didn't have time for such uselessness.

It was another gift from the goddess when she'd received a call from her FBI contact, telling her of Sebastian's intel as to where West was heading next.

She'd immediately made arrangements to get to

the temple at Philae. The organization had men on the ground near Aswan, mercenary soldiers who Leonid and Markos had contacted to help them. She was able to beat the feds here since she didn't have to go through protocol and chains of command that they did. As soon as her contact alerted her, she was in the air for the quick flight to Aswan.

Still, she knew she didn't have much time. The FBI would only be a couple of hours behind them.

"I don't have all day," Yara said now, pressing the weapon so firmly into Nick's temple that she saw him wince, though she knew he was doing everything in his power not to show pain.

"Adrian, don't tell—" he began.

Yara whipped the pistol across Nick's forehead, sending him sprawling to the ground. She took aim as if about to fire—

"Philae temple!" Adrian shouted. "We—we're going to the temple at Philae."

"Why?" Yara pressed.

"A hieroglyph we found at the ruins of Cleopatra's palace. We believe it's a clue leading her children to the temple, where she may have hid the treasure."

Yara studied her closely. From the desperation and fear in Adrian's eyes, she could tell that West was telling her the truth.

"Good. Now wasn't that easy?" Yara said, turning her pistol toward Adrian instead. "Let's all go together, shall we?"

CHAPTER 37

Philae Temple Complex
Agilkia Island, Egypt
6:42 P.M.

*W*ith the butt of a rifle pressed firmly into the small of her back, Adrian stepped out of the boat onto the island of Agilkia, where the ruins of the Philae temple complex stood, lit up against the inky darkness of the surrounding sky and waters of the Nile.

Adrian suspected that Yara had bribed some official to have the temple complex all to themselves. There wasn't any museum staff or security in sight.

Though fear had settled itself into the base of her spine, Adrian kept her pace steady, her gaze focused ahead, taking in the massive temple entranceway of the complex, majestic and impressive with two large lions carved in granite guarding its entrance. Julien flanked her as they walked past the entrance, a guard trailing him, his own rifle pressed to his back. Directly ahead of her, Yara walked next to Nick, her pistol aimed steadily at his head; Adrian knew it was her way of keeping her in check. She must have gleaned how important Nick was to her.

Adrian knew they *had* to find something of note at this temple or all three of them, not just Nick, would be dead. Figuring out how to keep the treasure out of Yara's hands would have to come later.

Right now, she just wanted to keep Julien and Nick alive. She could only pray that they'd followed the right clues leading them here.

They entered the forecourt, the main courtyard of the temple, the grounds now lit with modern lights, but Adrian could imagine what these sacred grounds must have looked like in ancient times, with its majestic colonnades lit by firelight.

"We should head into the temple of Isis and Hathor," Julien said. She could tell he was terrified, his voice wavering as he spoke, and a stab of guilt pierced her. She should have insisted that he stay behind with Sebastian back in Cairo. "If Cleopatra left a hidden message or something for her children to find, it will most likely be in that temple."

Yara turned, studying him for a long moment. "Let them look around," she ordered their guards.

"But you have my permission to shoot them if they try anything."

~

7:52 P.M.

ADRIAN COULD TELL that Yara was getting impatient.

She and Julien had thoroughly explored the temple dedicated to the goddess Isis and her son, Hathor. Like the courtyard, it was surrounded by colonnades, dotted with inscriptions by rulers from the Ptolemaic king Eurgetes II to the Roman emperor Tiberius, along with scenes of Horus and Isis. But they'd found nothing that even hinted at a secret message from Cleopatra.

They'd then made their way into an inner temple, this one filled with eight columns. The reliefs on these walls were filled with images of more gods and goddesses, including Horus, Isis and Nephthys, presenting the crowns of Lower and Upper Egypt.

Now they were in the temple of Isis. This temple featured small rooms with reliefs of the king in the presence of the goddess. Adrian and Julien were taking in every square inch of the images and writing on the temple walls, but again, she saw nothing indicating a secret message.

If there was nothing here, Adrian knew

they wouldn't find anything. The west side of this room led out to what used to be the gateway of Hadrian, which was built long after Cleopatra's time during the reign of the Roman emperor Hadrian. The other parts of the temple complex were also built beyond Cleopatra's time.

Think, she thought frantically. She could feel Yara's gaze boring into her and tried not to let her rising panic show. She met Julien's fear-filled gaze and knew exactly what he was thinking; there was nowhere else to search.

She had the foreboding feeling that they weren't in the right place.

"I think it's time to give you an incentive," Yara snapped, stepping forward. "I'm going to start at five. By the time I get to one, I want some kind of answer as to where the treasure is, or I kill your boyfriend. And then I kill Mr. Caron."

"Wait—" Adrian began, terrified.

"Five," Yara said.

Adrian turned to face the wall, ignoring the raging sound of her heartbeat, trying to focus.

Message for her children, something they would have known to look for. Somewhere safe.

She thought of the main courtyard, the rooms for the priests. Some could have been loyal followers of Cleopatra after her fall.

"Four," Yara said.

"The priests' rooms off the main courtyard—I need to look there."

"Fine, but the countdown continues once we get there," Yara snapped.

Adrian's throat was tight with terror as Yara and the guards marched her, Julien and Nick out to the main courtyard, toward the rooms on the west that the ancient priests used.

"Maybe one of the priests was loyal to Cleopatra and inscribed a message here, on behalf of the queen," Adrian said to Julien.

"Three," Yara said.

Julien was pale and shaking as he scanned every inch of the walls, Adrian at his side, but there was nothing. Nothing.

Terror gripping her, Adrian looked around the room, but there was nothing of note, nothing that stood out.

"Two," Yara said.

"Wait," Adrian said, holding up her hands as she turned to face Yara. "Give us more time, please. If you just—"

"Adrian," Nick interrupted. He held her gaze. Though he was pale, his expression was steady. "It's OK."

Anguish like she'd never known before flooded her body, and Adrian turned back to Yara, her eyes filling with tears of desperation.

"Just give me more time, and I will lead you—"

"You know what I think?" Yara hissed. "I think you don't have anything, which means you're no longer useful to me.

Yara turned to face Nick. "One."

Adrian screamed as a single gunshot fired out.

CHAPTER 38

8:03 P.M.

Fairuza had grown tired of Yara and her games.

When she'd joined the Daughters, she'd looked up to Yara with admiration, wanting so much to be like her. Yet over time, she'd realized that Yara was just as greedy and corrupt as the male-led governments she wanted to overthrow.

Fairuza knew she could do a better job. She *would* do a better job.

She'd wanted to wait until the treasure was found; that had been the plan all along. But when Yara had pressed her finger to the trigger, on the verge of recklessly murdering an American federal agent and losing the help they needed to find the treasure, she knew she had to act.

Fairuza raised her weapon in the air, firing off a single shot. This startled Yara, who whirled, lowering her pistol, but the other guards, most notably Leonid, knew that now was the time to act.

Two of the guards kept their weapons on Adrian, Julien and Nick, while the rest turned their weapons on Yara.

Fairuza took a moment to enjoy the look of abject astonishment on Yara's face. She'd clearly never imagined that quiet, skittish Fairuza could do such a thing, but she could now see Yara's dawning realization.

"What—what are you—" Yara began.

"Shut up," Fairuza said coolly. "One thing you used to always tell me was to not talk so damn much. So, for once, you will listen to me."

She moved forward until she was next to Leonid and pulled him in for a long kiss.

Everyone, including Leonid, knew that Yara was using him, but the difference between Yara and Fairuza was that she genuinely cared for Leonid.

She'd come up with her plan to take control of Daughters not long after Yara had obtained the artifacts; it was the same night that she and Leonid had become lovers. Leonid had become increasingly jealous of Yara's preference of his brother, Markos. It was easy to exploit his growing resentment of her.

It had taken a lot of quiet late-night meetings and secret flights, but she'd drummed up enough support in the organization that taking over was assured once she got her hands on Cleopatra's elusive treasure.

In the meantime, she'd continued to play Yara's fawning sycophant. She personally thought her tearful apology to Yara back on the plane was a nice touch. She'd played her part well.

"I want to thank you for your guidance," Fairuza said as a guard tied Yara's hands behind her back. "You also warned me to never trust anyone. I'll take over leadership of Daughters from this point forward. I wanted to wait until we had the treasure in hand, but attempting to kill Agent Harper is yet another example of your rashness and why you're not fit to lead. Adrian, you have my word," she continued, turning to look at Adrian, "that once you and your friends help us find the treasure, you're all free to go. Once we have some lead time to escape, of course. Does that sound like a deal, Miss West?"

"A better deal would be to let my friends go," Adrian snapped.

Fairuza clucked her lips but gave Adrian a look of admiration. "You're not exactly in a position to negotiate, but I like your courage. You would have been a fine recruit for Daughters."

"Maybe if I were a murderer," Adrian returned, her eyes flashing fire.

"Careful," Fairuza said, aiming her weapon at Adrian. "Now, I'm going to let you get to the business of solving where this treasure is, but I will not hesitate to harm you and your friends if necessary, though I *really* don't want to do that. Are we understood?"

Adrian gave her a shaky nod. "We—we need space to think," she said. "Do we need all the men with guns?"

"I may be friendlier than Yara, but I'm not stupid. I can, however, do *fewer* men with guns."

"I guess I have no choice."

"You don't." Fairuza turned to several of the guards. "Go outside, but stay close. Yara stays here. I don't trust her out of my sight."

ADRIAN STUDIED FAIRUZA, trying to think of how she could use this latest twist to her advantage.

Her heartbeat was still a battering ram against her chest; she was reeling over Yara nearly killing Nick. Nick and Julien looked just as shaken, but they were alive.

For now.

Concentrate, she ordered herself.

Young, reckless, thinks she's smarter than she is, Adrian thought, doing a quick profile of the young woman. Despite her criticism of Yara, what Fairuza had just done was incredibly rash. She'd given their prisoners a view of the cracks in Yara's group. Cracks that could buy them time and help them escape.

She wouldn't waste this opportunity.

"The key to all of this is Osiris," Adrian said. "I think we need to take another look at the relief of Osiris in the other temple."

"Adrian's right," Julien added. "We may have missed something."

"You can look, but I don't want to be here all night," Fairuza warned.

"Understood," Adrian said.

They made their way back to the inner temple with the relief of Osiris on the wall. She noticed with unease that Fairuza still had a guard training a gun at Nick's head. She would have to be very careful with this next play. She wouldn't allow harm to come to Nick. The anguish that tore through her when she thought Yara had pulled the trigger . . .

She took a shaky breath and stepped closer to the faded images, making a show of examining the wall. She then looked at the ground, tapping her foot along the base of the wall.

"Julien, come look at this," she said, feigning excitement.

Julien approached her, and she gave him a look. He hadn't known her for long, but he already seemed to understand the hidden meaning behind her look. *Play along*.

"How did we not notice this before?" Julien asked, playing his role to a tee.

"What?" Fairuza asked, stepping forward, her eyes shining with eagerness and greed.

Adrian continued to use her foot to tap along the base of the wall. "It feels more hollow here."

She looked up at Fairuza. Holding up her

hands, Adrian stepped back, gesturing for her to come forward. "Test it for yourself."

Fairuza stepped forward, testing the base of the relief with her foot. With the guards' focus on her, Adrian made her move.

She lunged forward and slammed Fairuza's head against the wall, sending her sprawling to the ground, dazed. She ducked out of the way as Leonid reached for her with a growl of fury.

Nick headbutted his guard, twisting out of his grasp and using the element of surprise to disarm him. He tackled Leonid from behind as Adrian leaned down to disarm Fairuza, firing at the two guards who approached them.

Nick successfully disarmed Leonid, shooting him in both legs.

As Fairuza's remaining guards entered the temple, raising their weapons to fire, Adrian, Nick, and Julien crouched low and darted toward the far exit to flee.

adrian, Nick, and Julien raced out of the temple. Yet as soon as they rounded the corridor—

Several more guards who'd been outside approached. They turned, racing toward the west side of the temple.

"There's a passageway off of the side of this temple!" Julien shouted.

They followed him as he scrambled toward a long stretch of wall off to the side of the temple. There, Adrian could make out the entrance to a very narrow passageway.

They made their way to it, ducking inside. As Julien and Adrian entered, Nick hovered behind, turning to face the approaching guards, readying his weapon.

"What are you doing?! Come on!" Adrian shouted.

"They'll just come after us—I'll be right behind you. Get the hell out of here!" Nick shouted.

Adrian hesitated, desperately not wanting to leave him behind, but he was right.

"Adrian, go now or you'll get us all killed!" Nick shouted, firing his weapon as the guards got closer.

Adrian forced herself to scramble through the passageway to the other side, which led to just outside of the temple complex where the outskirts of the island lay, the waves of the Nile lapping at the shore.

She and Julien ducked low, Adrian with her gun at the ready, as a barrage of gunfire sounded in the passageway behind them.

Adrian was on the verge of turning back to enter the passageway, Nick's order be damned, when he stumbled out, clutching his bleeding shoulder.

"I held them off—for now. Let's go!"

They remained low as they ran, trying to maintain their balance on the marshy shore.

"There's another set of steps that lead to the forecourt ahead on the right, toward the first pylon!" Julien shouted.

Keeping low, Adrian veered to the right, Nick and Julien on her tail, just as they heard two guards clamor after them from the passageway. She picked up her pace, and to her relief, she saw the steps up ahead. It would be tricky, but if they could dart through the courtyard and get to the boat, dispatching the guards there, they could get away.

They hurried up the steps and raced through the forecourt toward the first pylon as another set of guards approached.

Adrian and Nick fired at them as they ran; they were almost at the exit when a bullet struck Julien in the leg.

He let out a pained moan. Adrian and Nick turned back, helping him to his feet, putting their arms around him to heft him forward, but they'd already lost precious time. The guards quickly surrounded them, ordering them in Arabic to drop their weapons and get to their knees.

Despair and frustration filled Adrian. Still clutching Julien between them, Adrian and Nick obeyed.

Fairuza approached from the main entranceway of the temple complex, rubbing her temple, which now sported a bruise. She took in Adrian, shaking her head, looking more disappointed than angry.

"Oh, Adrian," she said with a heavy sigh. "I wanted us to work together. As misguided as Yara is, I was hoping she was wrong about you. But it looks like she wasn't. I'll be merciful. You get to die first."

Fairuza raised her pistol as Adrian braced herself to dodge, but a group of men raced into the complex and surrounded them, shouting at Fairuza and her men in both English and Arabic to drop their weapons.

Adrian turned, startled, as the men parted . . . and Briggs approached.

~

Agilkia Island, Egypt
10:15 P.M.

ADRIAN AND NICK sat on a boat that belonged to the local authorities, debriefing Briggs, Agent Farino, and Sebastian on everything that had happened.

Julien had been transported to a local hospital; he was shaken but in stable condition. His leg would heal just fine with time. Nick had refused to go to the hospital as the bullet that struck him had only grazed his shoulder. He'd had it carefully bandaged by a paramedic.

After Farino left to go question Fairuza and the others in custody, Briggs and Sebastian told them how they found them, with Briggs apologizing for initially suspecting her despite the other multiple layers of evidence.

"I was treating it like a cut-and-dry murder investigation, and that's never what it was. I am, however, still pissed at you for taking off," Briggs said, giving Nick a glare. "You could have stayed and talked some sense into me."

"Since when have you ever listened to me?"

Nick challenged, raising a brow.

"Fair enough," Briggs grunted, offering a hint of a smile. "We have Fairuza, Leonid, and their mercenaries in custody, but apparently Yara Elmasry escaped amidst the chaos. We have men scouting the entire island and boats along the Nile. She couldn't have gotten far."

Farino approached Briggs, murmuring something in his ear. "Give me a second," he said, giving them a polite nod before leaving.

Adrian looked out at the dark waters of the Nile, frustration surging through her. She was angered that Yara had escaped, and that the treasure had eluded them.

"Hey. You did the best you could. We all did," Nick said, seeming to read her mind. "And Yara couldn't have gotten far."

"If there was ever a treasure . . . it's long gone now. I've always known my theory was a long shot," Sebastian added.

"But the clues . . . " Adrian said, shaking her head. "They have to lead somewhere."

"I know. But this is something that's been hidden for centuries. Hell, we're still discovering items from ancient Egypt all the time, and there are things that will never be discovered. This treasure may very well be one of them. For me, it will have to be enough to know that Cleopatra fought longer and harder than history tells us."

Sebastian gave her a wistful smile, but she felt divided. She couldn't help the gnawing feeling that they were again missing something. And she hated leaving things unfinished, especially after everything they'd gone through up until this point.

She'd had the same feeling after her last case with the FBI, the one that had prompted her to resign. It was the case of a missing Georgia college student the bureau was tasked with helping the local authorities solve.

Adrian had pinpointed the young woman's location after doing a profile of her likely killer, but because of the bureau's protocols and turf wars with the local police department, they hadn't gotten to the location in time, and the young woman was found dead.

They eventually found her killer, but Adrian had never forgiven herself. It was the final straw of what had been her rising dissatisfaction with working for the FBI. She'd handed in her resignation the next day.

Now, as she looked out at the dark waters of the Nile, she couldn't help but feel that same lingering sense of failure.

CHAPTER 40

Aswan, Egypt
2:34 A.M.

"Adrian?" her mother asked, her voice filled with relief. "I'm so glad to hear from you. I was starting to get worried."

"Hey, Mom," Adrian said, trying to keep her tone light.

She was in her hotel room in Aswan, having just returned from visiting Julien in the local hospital. His injury was thankfully not serious, but the doctors wanted to keep him a few days to give his legs more time to heal and for observation.

After another debriefing session with Briggs and a late-night meal with Nick and Sebastian, she'd retired to her room.

Unable to sleep, she knew she might as well give her mother a call. It was long overdue.

"What's wrong, honey?" her mother pressed,

and Adrian knew her attempt at lightness had failed.

"Everything," Adrian said, and proceeded to tell her everything that had happened since that fateful night that Nick had called her in Rome, the story pouring out of her.

Her mother kept silent and listened even as she described some of the more dangerous parts of her journey, including the shootout at the temple in Philae.

"Now . . . we still have nothing. Sebastian's main abductor got away. And it just feels like we're missing something. We were so close," Adrian said, heaving a sigh.

"Do you remember that game we used to play with your father?" her mother asked. "The one where he'd have us solve a puzzle, but purposefully leave out several pieces?"

"Yeah," Adrian replied. Her father loved to play puzzle games with them and was oddly insistent on leaving out several pieces until the game was complete. *It forces you to see things from all angles,* he'd replied, whenever she or her mother complained. *Sometimes that's the best way to solve a problem.*

"All angles, remember?" her mother prodded.

"I remember," Adrian said. "Maybe I'll try that. I hated how he insisted on leaving out pieces. It only made the game harder." She paused, her voice wavering, as she continued, "I miss him."

"So do I, honey," her mother replied with a sigh. "So do I."

Adrian could still remember the circumstances of her father's disappearance like it was yesterday.

While researching for a book he was writing on the origins of proto-Indo-European languages, he'd traveled to Istanbul, where he'd simply . . . vanished. He was last seen leaving the airport in Istanbul, and after that, his trail went cold.

Adrian had flown to Istanbul to attempt to find him, only to find the local authorities not helpful. There were no witnesses, no evidence as to what happened to him. Authorities informed her he was likely robbed and left for dead, and his body simply hadn't been found.

Though logic told her he was likely dead, his disappearance was still an open wound, an unanswered question she and her mother would have to live with for the rest of their lives.

This had driven her to join the FBI, to answer questions for other families that would never be answered for hers. Perhaps in her own way, every case she'd solved while with the bureau had been a temporary panacea for the pain of never finding her father.

Adrian and her mother spoke some more, with her mother admonishing her to please be careful. Before they ended the call, her mother asked, hesitantly, "Does this adventure mean you're going back into law enforcement?"

If her mother had asked her that weeks ago,

Adrian's answer automatically would have been no. Yet despite the danger she'd been in, she'd felt herself come alive over the past few days as if she were awakening from a long slumber.

"I don't know," Adrian said finally.

There was another long pause, and Adrian waited tensely, remembering her mother's reaction when she'd first decided to join the bureau.

"Well, whatever you decide," her mother said. "I'll support you."

"Thanks," Adrian said, surprised at how much she needed to hear those words.

Adrian hung up, considering what her mother had told her. *All angles.*

But what angle was she missing?

She moved over to the table. Briggs had an agent lend her one of their laptops. She opened it, searching online for a map of the Philae temple complex and the area surrounding it.

All angles.

The hieroglyph had pointed to Osiris. And she knew that Upper Egypt was a sanctuary for Cleopatra and her followers. Was there anything else related to Osiris in the area?

She searched for Osiris temples in the area, and another small island popped up.

The island of Bigeh, close to the Philae temple complex. She drummed her fingers on the desk before picking up her phone and dialing the number for Sebastian's room.

He picked up at the first ring, chuckling into her ear. "I take it you couldn't sleep either."

"No," she said with a sigh, still staring at the image of the island of Bigeh on her screen. "Can you tell me what you know about the island of Bigeh?"

"It was also believed to be a burial place of Osiris by the ancient Egyptians," Sebastian said slowly. "But it doesn't get nearly the attention that the Philae temple complex does."

Adrian's heart picked up its pace. From what she could glean about it online, though Bigeh was larger, it was not nearly as trafficked as Philae—in both ancient and modern times. It would have been a better and safer place to hide a treasure.

"Are we thinking the same thing?" Sebastian asked.

"We are," Adrian said. "I'm calling Nick and Agent Briggs."

Bigeh Island, Egypt
9:02 A.M.

ADRIAN STOOD NEXT TO NICK, Sebastian and Briggs as she walked around the ruins of the old temple in Bigeh.

After she'd spoken to Briggs, the local authorities had put him in touch with two local archaeologists, who were insistent that the area around the ancient temple on Bigeh had been thoroughly excavated.

Adrian had wanted to come here anyway. Her gut told her that Bigeh could be the piece they were missing.

"What about the rest of the island?" she asked one of the archaeologists.

"Our focus in recent times has been on the temple," he replied stiffly. She could tell that he and the other archaeologist were annoyed with her. They were right to be. They knew this island better than she did.

Still. *All angles.*

She stepped away from their group, her gaze sweeping over the island. In the distance, she noticed several locals heading toward their homes. She turned to look at Briggs.

"Can you do me a favor?" she asked.

Moments later, Adrian and Nick sat huddled outside the home of a local man named Ahmed, drinking cups of hibiscus tea that he'd kindly offered them. Briggs had one of the local archaeologists introduce her to him at her request. After they exchanged pleasantries in Arabic, Adrian switched topics.

"I wanted to talk to you because I have a question," she said. "Is there anything in your oral tradition about an area of the island that has been left untouched? Since ancient times?"

If there was anything ancient hidden on the island, the people who would be the most aware of it were the Nubian locals, who had inhabited the island, and the region since antiquity.

Ahmed didn't look surprised by her question. He held up a hand and politely told her to wait before going into his home. Several moments later, he came out with an elderly man, introducing him as his grandfather. Ahmed repeated her question to his grandfather, whose eyes lit up.

The old man stood, hobbling several feet ahead, pointed to a crumbling old stone building on the north part of the island.

"That area," he said in clear Arabic, "has been untouched for many years. My great-grandfather told me that the sacred gift of the queen was left there."

CHAPTER 41

Aswan, Egypt
Twelve Hours Ago

arkos placed his hand on Yara's shoulder as she sat in an armchair overlooking the small courtyard of the house they were staying in. Even his soothing hand on her shoulder didn't alleviate her tension. She was still reeling with shock over Fairuza's betrayal, and rage filled her at how everything had fallen apart.

The woman whose home she was staying in, Djamila, entered, her head bowed reverently, handing Yara a cup of mint tea. Yara's instinct was to refuse it, to throw it in Djamila's face in case it was poisoned . . . but she had offered them sanctuary and was a loyal Daughter's member.

Or was she? After Fairuza's betrayal, she didn't know who to trust.

Finally, she took it with a nod of her head.

Yara had managed to escape the shootout at the temple by fleeing on her waiting boat, where Markos was waiting for her. She'd feared he was working with Fairuza, and had pointed a gun she'd taken from one of Fairuza's guards at him, but he'd held up his hands and assured her he had nothing to do with the plot.

"We need to leave—now," he'd insisted.

She'd had no choice but to trust him in the moment, yet kept her gun trained on him as he sped the boat away from the island and toward Aswan.

There, with Yara's face mostly covered with a scarf, they'd taken a taxi to Djamila's home in central Aswan. Yara had been wary of trusting Djamila, but she didn't have much choice but to hide here. The authorities were looking for her.

She could at least take small comfort in the fact that Fairuza and Leonid's plan hadn't worked, and they'd been captured. Markos had told her it was wise to flee Egypt altogether for now and regroup, to determine who was still on her side in the organization, but Yara couldn't do that. Even if the treasure wasn't at Philae temple, it was close. She could feel it.

She had her FBI contact keeping surveillance on Adrian; he'd informed her they were decamped at a hotel in Aswan while Julien was staying overnight in a local hospital.

She suspected that if any progress was to be made with finding the treasure, it would be through

Adrian West. In West, she recognized the same dog-eyed perseverance she had. West wanted the treasure as badly as Yara did. Maybe for different reasons, but she had the feeling that nothing would stop her.

Yara didn't sleep that night, her eyes trained on the ceiling of the pathetically tiny guest bedroom she was staying in. She knew she should, but all her focus wavered between the location of the treasure and her foolishness over trusting—even caring—for Fairuza.

Never would she make that mistake again.

The early morning light was pouring in through the windows and Yara's eyes had just begun to grow heavy as Markos entered, offering her a rare smile.

"Finally, some good news," he said. "You were right about West—she must know something. Your contact just called. The FBI and locals are doing a dig on Bigeh Island."

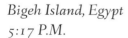

Bigeh Island, Egypt
5:17 P.M.

ADRIAN HOVERED as a group of local professional diggers, directed by Sebastian and the archaeologists, dug in the area that Ahmed's grandfather had pointed out to her.

They'd already been here for two hours, and

the longer the diggers worked with no find, the less hope she had. Nick stood at her side, his eyes intently on the diggers as they worked; he looked as tense as she felt.

There was a sudden shout and Adrian turned. One digger had struck something and gestured for Sebastian to come forward. Sebastian looked down at what the man had discovered before frantically waving for Adrian and Nick to come over.

The man had uncovered a sealed wooden box, worn with age. He carefully lifted it, handing it to Sebastian.

A heavy, momentous silence fell over the group as Sebastian used the edge of a trowel to carefully pry open the box.

"My God," he whispered.

Inside the box were fragments of papyrus, and there were faint traces of writing on it.

Sebastian used a digital microscope to read aloud the words that he could make out.

"Sun . . . moon," he said slowly. "Home of Chera." He lowered the microscope, his face taut with emotion as he met Adrian's eyes, before reading the final word. "India."

CHAPTER 42

Ananganadi Hills
Karur, India
12:32 P.M.

he Ananganadi Hills, located just outside of Karur, India, were tucked away on a stretch of mountain popular for hikers and nature watchers with its rich greenery and wildlife.

It was also—possibly—the location of Cleopatra's tomb.

Adrian ventured into the caverns tucked away in the remote section of the hills, far from the more touristy section. Nick, Sebastian, and a local team comprising of five archaeologists accompanied her. Briggs, agents from the Cairo FBI office, and the local police were gathered outside of the entrance to the caverns.

Given the historical and cultural significance of

the potential find, the authorities had wanted to send in even more people, from law enforcement to historians, but Sebastian and the local archaeologists had cautioned them against this. If there were a tomb tucked away in the mountains, it was in an extremely delicate state and too many people in it at once could cause the site unnecessary disturbance.

It was so silent that Adrian could only hear the furious pounding of her heartbeat. She could practically taste the sense of anticipation in the air as they ventured toward what she hoped was Cleopatra's long-lost tomb . . . and her hidden treasure.

The FBI's tech team in Rome and Cairo—spearheaded by Vince, who kept insisting that Nick owed him a bar after helping them back in Italy—had used a combination of ground-penetrating radar and geophysical mapping to zero in on a location in the mountains outside of Karur, India. The location was near an old palace, now lost to time, that once belonged to the Chera royal family of India.

"The Chera family in India traded with the Ptolemies; they had diplomatic ties. Other historians and I believe that Cleopatra perhaps planned to marry off her children to members of the royal family, hence her sending off Caesarion to India around the time of her fall," Sebastian had told her.

The radar had detected a hollowed-out chasm located deep within the mountains that didn't seem natural; it would be the perfect place to conceal a tomb . . . and treasure. Upon this discovery, they'd moved quickly, getting the local authorities in Karur onboard; they had provided them with the team of archaeologists who accompanied them now, they were familiar with the mountains surrounding Kerala.

Because of the treacherous nature of venturing into a largely unexplored stretch of mountain caverns, they all wore helmets outfitted with flash-lights. She didn't know how long they walked—it seemed like at least a couple of hours—when one of the archaeologists, a young woman by the name of Priya, stopped and pointed straight ahead.

"We're close. The area the radar detected is roughly one hundred meters ahead."

Adrian nodded, meeting Sebastian's and Nick's eyes. It was surreal that they were possibly on the verge of entering the tomb of history's most famous queen. She could see the emotion in Sebastian's eyes and instinctively reached out to squeeze his hand. He had been through so much; he deserved this discovery.

They continued forward, halting when the muffled sound of an explosion went off in the distance. Adrian whirled toward the sound of gunfire, reaching for the holstered weapon she had been provided by the local police.

"Get behind us!" Adrian shouted to Sebastian and the archaeologists as Nick took out his own gun.

Looking fearful, Sebastian and the others

obliged. Adrian could hear the sounds of footsteps approaching and voices speaking a combination of Arabic and Tamil, the local tongue. Panic rose within her, and she turned to Priya.

"Is there somewhere within these caverns for you and the others to hide?"

"There—there are some crawlspaces up ahead," Priya said shakily.

"Go," Nick said sharply. "Now."

"And no matter what you hear, don't come out," Adrian added. Sebastian looked as if he was about to protest, but at her look, he fell silent.

As soon as Sebastian, Priya, and the others had darted farther into the caverns, Nick and Adrian cautiously moved forward, their weapons at the ready, adrenaline pumping through her veins.

She had the uneasy feeling that this latest attack was because of Yara. If Cleopatra's tomb and the treasure were here, she wouldn't let Yara get near it.

The footsteps grew closer. Adrian and Nick pressed themselves into the shadows of the cavern wall, tucking their bodies into a large crevasse.

After several tense moments, Adrian saw a half-dozen heavily armed men, reminding her eerily of the men who'd surrounded them in Aswan, followed by Yara and the broad-shouldered man she recognized from the farmhouse and back in Aswan—Markos.

Fury spreading through her, Adrian pressed

herself deeper into the crevasse, raising her weapon and aiming it at Yara. She fired off a single shot.

But Markos darted in front of Yara, taking the bullet to his chest. He sank to the ground, still, blood soaking the area around him.

Yara whirled toward them, and the armed men rushed forward, rifles at the ready as Adrian and Nick stepped out of the shadows, lifting their weapons—

"Stop!" Yara shouted, raising a pistol and pointing it right at Adrian's heart.

Adrian and Nick froze. Yara's men held their fire but kept their weapons trained on Adrian and Nick.

Yara approached Adrian, fury and determination in her gaze, not stopping until she stood before her, pressing the barrel of her pistol hard into Adrian's chest.

"You're taking me to Cleopatra's tomb. Or I can find Sebastian and those archaeologists and start executing them one by one, and then Agent Harper. It's your choice."

Fear and frustration surged through Adrian's chest, knowing she was defeated. They'd been so close. She could tell by Yara's expression that she would eagerly carry out her threat.

She gave Yara a jerky nod of assent. Yara forced her forward, keeping the gun jammed into her back. "Walk."

ADRIAN MOVED DEEPER into the caverns.

Yara was her shadow, her gun painful against the small of her back. Unlike before, she now only felt dread. If the treasure was where Priya had said it would be, and Yara got her hands on it . . .

She took a breath, tamping down her dread, continuing to move forward. Nick was at her side, another guard's rifle pressed into his back. Yara had ordered him to shoot Nick if Adrian so much as took a faltering step.

Tension crawled the walls of the silence as they continued forward, until they reached what appeared to be the entrance of another cavern, sealed off with a makeshift door of granite. If Priya hadn't mentioned the location, she would have walked right past it. The granite door blended in with the cavernous wall surrounding it. In this unexplored section of mountain, it was no wonder it had never been found.

Her dread and anticipation spiked. This had to be it. The entrance to Cleopatra's tomb.

Yara nodded to her mercenaries, who moved forward, and with great effort, they pushed aside the granite door.

Two of the mercenaries flicked on their flash-lights. As the cavern within was revealed, Adrian went stiff with amazement.

CHAPTER 43

2:15 P.M.

*B*efore them lay rickety a set of crumbling stone stairs, leading into a cavernous room.

A room that was filled to the brim with treasure.

And in the very center, a golden sarcophagus, glinting in the dim light.

It was all here. The treasure . . . and Cleopatra.

"Thank you, goddess," Yara whispered from behind her.

She pushed Adrian forward. Adrian had to fight to maintain her balance as she made her way carefully down the stairs, using her helmet light and the guards' flashlights as illumination.

Once they reached the bottom of the stairs, Adrian took it all in. Layers of dust and grime covered every square inch of the room; this was a place that had not been disturbed for centuries. But none of that could lessen the splendor of the treasure that lay before them.

There were stacks of gold, silver, and carved ivory, statuary made of alabaster, ivory and gold. Chests stuffed to the brim with gold coins, pearls and semiprecious stones—garnet, topaz, malachite, agate, lapis, amethyst, carnelian. There was jewelry, from pendants to bracelets to earrings, inlaid with these stones. And in the far corner of the room, there were life-sized golden statues of Cleopatra and Marc Antony.

Yara stepped forward reverently, seeming to forget all about Adrian. Even her men looked awestruck, though they kept their rifles trained on Nick and Adrian.

Adrian slid a glance at Nick. As amazing as it was to be in Cleopatra's tomb, they needed to act fast. Now that they'd found the treasure, Yara would have no use for them.

Before she could decide on a plan of action, she saw a movement out of the corner of her eye, and astonishment filled her.

It was Sebastian, who had crawled out from behind the statue of Cleopatra and Mark Antony, tucked away in the far corner of the room. He lunged toward one of the armed men whose back was turned toward him, brandishing a small alabaster statue as a weapon. Priya and the other archaeologists moved out from other hidden positions, lunging toward the men with makeshift weapons of their own. The other guards, stunned, whirled to face them.

Adrian and Nick immediately sprang into action.

Adrian darted toward Yara, while Nick whirled on the man who guarded him, his rifle going off as they struggled with it.

Adrian tackled Yara to the ground just as she turned around. With a ferocious snarl, Yara maneuvered onto her back, raising her weapon to fire—

But Adrian wrapped her hands around the barrel of her gun, keeping it pointed away from her as they struggled.

Behind them, she could hear the sounds of grunts and gunshots as Nick and the others struggled with Yara's men.

Yara was strong for such a petite woman, and it took all of Adrian's strength to keep the gun pointed away from her.

Yara twisted, turning the gun to squeeze off a shot, but Adrian pressed the gun back down, hard, into Yara's chest, gritting her teeth with effort as she pulled the trigger.

Yara stilled, her eyes widening with surprise and shock. The bullet had entered her chest cavity, and blood soaked the ground around her body.

Adrian could see the life draining from Yara's eyes. Yara tore her eyes away from Adrian's to focus on Cleopatra's sarcophagus, keeping it trained there, until the light in her eyes finally went dim.

.

～

Cleopatra's Tomb
7:30 *P.M.*

PRIYA and the other archaeologists moved carefully through the room, taking photographs and cataloging every piece of treasure.

The entrance to the tomb had been roped off, and just outside Briggs was gathered with the local authorities.

Three of Yara's mercenaries were dead; the other two were now in custody. After the local coroner's office had carried out Yara and the bodies of her men, the tomb had been closed off once more. It would be weeks of bureaucracy as the items in the tomb, including Cleopatra's sarcophagus, were studied, catalogued, and eventually returned to Egypt.

Adrian, Nick and Sebastian had been debriefed by Briggs, who told them Yara's team had gotten in by using a separate entrance. They had put explosives at the main entrance to prevent the authorities from getting in while they attacked.

"And we had a mole," he'd told them, his face tight with anger. "The agent I've been working with this whole time, Agent Andrews."

"Andrews?" Nick echoed in surprise.

"He's been sleeping with a Daughters' member and giving Yara information. They were paying him off. I'd been wondering how confidential information was getting out and had Vince do an off-the-books search of phone records of agents on the case. We traced Andrews' calls to a number belonging to Yara. He's in custody now. Agent Farino—who used to be very skeptical of the Daughters' even existing—is now spearheading a task force to root out other members of this organization."

After their debriefing, Adrian, Sebastian and Nick had returned to the tomb. They would soon have to leave to allow the archaeologists to work; they wanted to have a moment alone with Cleopatra's remains before they were released to the world.

Together, they approached the sarcophagus in silent reverence.

"Alexander the Great's sarcophagus was originally gold. One of Cleopatra's ancestors sold it for war money, so in Cleopatra's time, his tomb was encased in glass, or alabaster. I think she was making a statement, linking herself to him . . . the first Greek to assert power over Egypt, to establish the Ptolemaic dynasty. She didn't know she'd be the last one."

They stood in silence for several long moments, gazing down at the sarcophagus.

Adrian allowed herself to imagine what would have happened had Cleopatra succeeded, and a new Hellenistic age dawned, an Egypt with more parity for men and women, less militaristic and patriarchal than Rome's society. How different would the world have been had Cleopatra succeeded in her plans?

She could understand the Daughters' original intention in ancient times right after their queen's defeat to restore her to power and overthrow tyranny.

But she could never understand the modern organization's turn to violence, all in the name of the queen who lay before them. She doubted that Cleopatra, even as shrewd and ruthless as she'd been, would have approved. Her strength had lain in diplomacy and will, in strength and alliance . . . not death and destruction.

Soon, it was time to leave. Sebastian and Nick headed out, but Adrian lingered. She placed her hand on the sarcophagus, paying her own silent tribute to Cleopatra before turning to follow them out.

CHAPTER 44

Three Weeks Later
Alexandria, Virginia
3:47 P.M.

*A*drian walked arm in arm with her mother through the cemetery.

It was a lovely day: the sky a pristine blue, the leaves of the surrounding trees sporting a vibrant green color. It ironically seemed as if the days were always lovely whenever she or her mother visited her father's headstone.

"Adrian," her mother hissed suddenly. "Look."

Adrian instinctively stiffened, following her mother's gaze through the trees. She relaxed, though annoyance skittered through her.

It was just another photographer.

After the explosive discovery of Cleopatra's tomb and treasure, Adrian, Nick, Julien and Sebastian had catapulted into an odd sort of fame with reporters wanting to interview them. Though Julien hadn't been physically with them when they discovered the treasure, Adrian and the others had been quick to give him the credit he deserved.

Julien, already popular, had welcomed the attention. The last time they'd spoken, he'd told her that his following had exploded by leaps and bounds; he'd even been offered his own archeological show on a history channel in both the United Kingdom and the States.

As for Adrian, Nick, and Sebastian, they had kept low profiles. Sebastian had granted interviews to scholarly outfits only, while Adrian and Nick had declined all interviews . . . which seemed to make journalists even more curious about them. That meant sneaky photographers who'd occasionally pop up out of nowhere to snap shots of the "renegade" former FBI agent who'd made the discovery of a lifetime.

She just wanted to know when her fifteen minutes of fame would be over already.

In the aftermath of the discovery, the artifacts Yara had stolen were returned, and a team of excavators, archaeologists and historians were carefully combing over every inch of Cleopatra's heavily guarded tomb, which had become a tourist attraction.

Adrian, Nick, Sebastian and Julien had gotten to be present as guests of honor when Cleopatra's mummified form was unveiled, which was both thrilling and surreal. The ancient queen had been delicate and petite. It amazed her that such a physically small woman had cast such a large shadow in both her time and throughout history.

Sebastian and Julien had been flying back and forth to India to help consult; Sebastian could barely contain his excitement whenever he told her of the progress the team was making.

While Adrian was happy with how everything had turned out, ever since she'd returned to the States, a restlessness had tugged at her. She'd once convinced herself that she was content with her life and career in academia, but after her rescue of Sebastian and pursuit of Cleopatra's treasure, she realized just how much she'd missed the thrill of investigation and discovery, the joy of saving lives. Though she'd returned to her lecturer position at NYU, she craved more adventure . . . another thrilling mystery to solve.

When they reached her father's headstone, Adrian placed down the flowers they'd brought, reaching out to take her mother's hand. They'd reluctantly purchased a headstone several years ago and had a memorial service, though it never felt right without her father's remains. Still, it had provided them with a small bit of closure.

"He would have been proud of you, honey," her mother said. "I know it."

Adrian just smiled, squeezing her hand. "I hope so."

As they made their way back to her mother's

car, she stiffened when she saw a male figure hovering by it, angry at the thought of it being that pesky photographer.

But as they drew closer, a ripple of delight went through her when she saw who it was. Nick.

Her mother, who had always adored Nick, brightened, moving forward to embrace him.

"Nick! It's so good to see you," she said. "We were just going back to the house for dinner. Why don't you join us?"

"I'd love to," Nick said, his gaze flicking to Adrian. "But if you don't mind, I'd like to have a brief word with your daughter alone first. I can give her a ride."

"Of course," her mother said, beaming. "I'll see you both at the house."

Nick and Adrian waited as her mother got into her car and drove off.

Adrian turned to face him, surprised at the depths of her joy at seeing him. They'd kept in touch sporadically since returning from India, with their friendship seeming to hang in the balance. Adrian had made more of an effort to keep in touch, but Nick hadn't been as responsive. She told herself it would take time to get back to the place they'd been . . . if they could ever get there. Still, his distance had hurt.

"I'm sorry I haven't been in touch as much," he said, seeming as he always did to read her mind. "I've been brought in on a new case."

"Oh," Adrian replied, envious at the knowledge

that Nick was taking on another investigation. "In art crimes?"

"Sort of," he replied cryptically. "It's in the UK, so I've been flying back and forth. Briggs put me on the case, but it's looking to be more complex than I thought. Briggs told me I could bring in anyone I wanted to consult. Your name *may* have come up."

Adrian's heart picked up its pace, anticipation flooding her. Nick sensed her growing delight, giving her a grin that enhanced his handsome features.

"How about it, West?" he asked. "Want to go on another adventure?"

～

The adventure continues in Book Two, THE EXCALIBUR DECEPTION.

AUTHOR'S NOTE

Like many, I've always found Cleopatra endlessly fascinating, this powerful ancient queen who was both the ally and enemy of Rome, who had children with two of its most powerful men—Julius Caesar and Marc Antony—and then had a spectacular fall.

It was this fall, much of which still remains shrouded in mystery, which led to the concept of this novel.

Rome was the victor over Cleopatra and her story, and as we know with history, its victors often get to tell their side of the story. I wanted to fill in the missing pieces of the end of Cleopatra's life with both what is known and unknown from history.

Let's start with the facts. As of this writing, Cleopatra's tomb remains undiscovered.

Cleopatra was survived by her children, though the boys soon perished—Caesarion and Alexander

Helios, whose deaths were likely ordered by or linked to Octavian turned Emperor Augustus himself, and Ptolemy Philadelphus, possibly of illness.

Her daughter, Cleopatra Selene, survived into adulthood, marrying King Juba and even establishing somewhat of a recreation of her mother's court in her new home after Rome, Mauretania. She did spend time in Rome after her mother's death, where she and her brother lived as wards of Augustus' sister, Octavia.

While the discovery of jewelry—including an amethyst ring that becomes crucial to the plot—belonging to her in Rome was invented for the novel, there is an actual amethyst ring referenced in antiquity that Cleopatra wore . . . but it has never been discovered.

And now for fact versus fiction. Though it is probable that there were many still loyal to Cleopatra after her fall, especially in Upper Egypt (now southern Egypt), the Daughters of Cleopatra secret society is entirely my invention.

It's not impossible that there is a hidden treasure out there somewhere yet to be discovered—there is historical reference to Cleopatra spiriting away treasure from her mausoleum at the end of her life. And with the Ptolemies' control of the rich Egyptian economy, they were incredibly, *incredibly* wealthy (my estimates in the novel are stingy, Cleopatra would have easily been considered a billionaire today).

While the ruins of Cleopatra's palace do indeed lie beneath the waters of the Mediterranean, the statue of the goddess Isis with the Osiris inscription was entirely my invention. There are still excavations being carried out at the site of ancient Pelusium, now an archaeological site and tourist attraction, as mentioned in the novel, but the discovery my characters pursue to El Qantara (and the fictional museum there) is also my invention.

The Philae temple complex, a place which I've had the distinct honor of visiting, exists and is truly stunning to behold. Bigeh Island also exists, it's the lesser visited island not far from the Philae temple, but was also very important to the Egyptians of antiquity.

My choosing of Cleopatra's tomb and treasure being hidden away in India does have a basis in history. We know that she sent her son Caesarion to India for safety, and it was one of the places she considered fleeing to after her fall. The Ptolemies did indeed have connections with the Chera royal family in India, they traded with them and it was likely that Cleopatra considered marrying her children into the family.

For research, I read countless articles and books about Cleopatra's life and the Ptolemies as a whole. Several of my most helpful sources—and highly recommended reading—include *Cleopatra, A Life*, by Stacey Schiff (the audiobook is divine), *Cleopatra, Last Queen of Egypt* by Joyce Tyldesley and *Cleopatra: A Biography* by Duane Roller.

I hope you've enjoyed taking this adventure with Adrian, Nick . . . and me! Stay tuned for more of Adrian's adventures—she's just getting started.

—L.D.G.
Paris, France
2021

ABOUT THE AUTHOR

L.D. Goffigan writes fast-paced thrillers and action-adventure with historical intrigue. She studied film and dramatic writing at New York University and currently divides her time between Paris, France and Los Angeles, California.

When not writing, you can find her traveling to places she's never been, reading the latest book which strikes her fancy, or watching a documentary about ancient mysteries.

To be notified about new releases, sign up for her newsletter on her website. Subscribers are also alerted to giveaways and exclusive bonus content.

Stay in touch!
ld@ldgoffiganbooks.com
ldgoffiganbooks.com

Made in the USA
Middletown, DE
13 July 2022